WYLDBLOOD
MAGAZINE

G000153577

Contents

Publisher:
Wyldblood Press,
Thicket View, Bakers Lane,
Maidenhead
SL6 6PX UK

Editor: Mark Bilsborough
Fiction editor Sandra Baker
First readers:
Vaughan Stanger
Mike Lewis
Rebecca Ruvinsky

Subscriptions: 6 issues epub/mobi/pdf delivered to your inbox £15.
6 issue print subscriptions £35
www.wyldblood.com/magazine.

Single issues available worldwide via Amazon and from Wyldblood.

www.wyldblood.com
contact@wyldblood.com
facebook.com/WyldbloodPress
t: @WyldbloodPress

Submissions: we are regularly open for submissions for flash fiction, short stories and novels – check our website for our current status and requirements. We are a paying market.

Issue 4 available to pre-order now – published July 2021
www.wyldblood.com/magazine

We need people to review us, and people to review *for* us.
Email mark@wyldblood.com

ISBN: 978-1-914417-02-3

Editorial

Welcome to issue 3 of Wyldblood Magazine, where we've got all manner of wonders to delight and unnerve you. We've got a mix of science fiction, fantasy and horror in our eight stories this time around so there should be something for everyone.

It's been a busy few months in the Wyldblood offices. Not only have we put out our first three issues of the magazine, but we've published our first anthology, *Call of the Wyld*, packed with werewolves getting up to all sorts of gory werewolfness in all sorts of unexpected places (werewolves on the moon?). We're also on Wyld Flash 42 and counting – that's our weekly serving of flash fiction, free on our website. Plus we've been quietly publishing a string of classic fiction – HG Wells' *The Island of Dr Moreau*, the *Legendary Conan the Barbarian*, *Classic Gothic* and many others – and are gearing up to publish our first original novels.

Our next anthology will be a steampunk one, *Runs Like Clockwork*, which we hope to publish before Christmas. We've had a phenomenal response to our call for submissions so we'll be spending the summer making some very tough choices.

Along with the stories in this issue we've got a short Steampunk piece to get you in the mood for the anthology and a couple of review features – books and TV/film. It's quite common for a magazine like ours to include book reviews (but should we? Let us know) but less so for TV and film. It's in here because speculative fiction is a multi-media thing these days (and has been for a long, long time) and I'm assuming that all you bibliophiles also watch TV, play games, read (or have read) comics and go to see movies from time to time. And I'm also assuming that if you enjoy the book, you'll be interested to see how it's breaking out all over the place. *Game of Thrones* and *The Expanse* make for excellent TV (barring the odd dodgy final episode) but their origins are firmly in printed form. I take the view that their different forms feed off each other and are aspects of the same idea-set, so I'm assuming you'll all be interested in anything current – am I wrong? Maybe you look to other places for news on the flickering world. But unless you tell us otherwise you'll be hearing about the upcoming *Dune* film, the promised *Foundation* series and the big budget *Lord of the Rings* adaptation, plus anything else that makes us reach for the popcorn.

I'm looking forward to *Foundation*, (out later this year on Apple TV+) because it's one of the books that got me into science fiction in the first place, back in the day. The idea that a planet-sized supercomputer and a brilliant mind could somehow accurately predict the future of mankind, just like the weather, was far-fetched back in the 1950s (though, I suspect, less so now) and it will be interesting to see how far the filmmakers stick to Asimov's blueprint. *Dune* is a harder sell for me, because I didn't like the Frank Herbert source book (I appreciate I'm an outlier in this but I couldn't warm to the writing style and I got bored with all the trade politics). The odd 2004 David Lynch film didn't help either – but I'm hopeful. And although I'm not surprised Amazon is pouring money into *Lord of the Rings* given the movie grosses I can't help but wonder if we actually need a *Rings* series. I am, though, open to being awestruck.

Lastly, back to books, the 2021 Hugo Awards nominations are out, so if you need some good summer reading try one or all of this lot:

- *Black Sun*, Rebecca Roanhorse
- *The City We Became*, N.K. Jemisin
- *Harrow The Ninth*, Tamsyn Muir
- *Network Effect*, Martha Wells
- *Piranesi*, Susanna Clarke
- *The Relentless Moon*, Mary Robinette Kowal

I hope you enjoy this issue – if you do, tell a friend, write a review or email us your thoughts – we'd love to hear from you. Enjoy the stories,

Mark

Run, Heloisa
David McGillveray

"You know the way, Heloisa."

They laughed as they threw her out of the back of the van. She sprawled in the dirt, spat dust and was up and running before the van screeched away, sprinting across the abandoned football field. A few shots rang out from somewhere but they were half-hearted, fired into the air. Just boys showing off.

She vaulted the low wall where graffiti covered the faded remnants of advertisements for liquor and tobacco and disappeared into the lowest level of the favela. The slums grew up the mountain like an infection, a jumble of terraces and multi-coloured hovels piled on top of one another. She glanced at the summit. It was wreathed in low morning cloud like a cut-price Olympus.

She tore between makeshift homes built from corrugated iron and crumbling concrete, stolen plastic sheeting and whatever the people could find to build with. Jungles of satellite dishes and aerials, power cables, solar panels and knots of fibre optics covered the rooftops. She splashed through filthy water in the street where open drains had overflowed, struggled up near vertical steps cut into the hillside.

Always upward. The only chance to live was to climb; those were the rules. Already, her breath burned in her chest.

She smelled sewage and chemicals and somewhere, something burning. Fire could spread quickly here, especially now there was no one to put it out.

It was strange to be back in this place. Even more bizarre now this part of the favela, usually so full of people, where families lived ten to a room and lived their whole lives in these tiny streets were all gone, cleared out for the day's entertainment by the gang's soldiers. Silence replaced the sounds of laughter and despair and every emotion inbetween. And the music. Where was the music? It used to pump from every doorway, sound systems and radios and voices and drums making a million rhythms. All she could hear now was the pounding of her boots and her heart.

They hadn't fed her since they abducted her off the street in Leblon the day before and after minutes of breakneck progress she began to feel light-headed. She paused in the shadows on the high side of the street she found herself in, looking around wildly for signs her hunters had found her already. Satisfied, she peered through a filthy plastic sheet that served for a window in the nearest shack. In its single room she could see mattresses pushed up against one wall, a small stove, a battered table.

Heloisa breathed out slowly. She was in luck. On a narrow worktop lay a knife next to half a brown apple and some bananas abandoned when the family was ordered out. She pushed through the plasterboard door and pushed one of the bananas hungrily into her mouth, slurping water from a jug she found.

She whirled at a tiny noise behind her, snatching up the knife and dropping into a crouch. She squinted in the dim light inside the shack until she made out the shape of a young boy hiding under the room's only table. His face peeped out from the blanket he had wrapped himself in.

Heloisa relaxed and slipped the knife into her belt. The boy looked no older than eleven, a cap of black hair brushed down over his forehead above big brown eyes and good cheeckbones. She whispered, "What are you doing here? They were meant to have cleared the whole place."

The boy stared at her for a long moment before managing to speak. "D-Dare," he squeaked at last.

"A dare?" she said through the last of the banana. "That's very stupid. You know if the dogs find you here they'll tear you apart."

His eyes opened even wider.

She wagged a finger. "It's true," she said, then, "Shhhh!"

She went to listen at the open door, holding out a hand behind her to silence the boy. From along the narrow street outside she could hear the hum of a drone. She pushed the door closed as quietly as she could and sank down behind it. The humming got louder as the machine approached, working its way through the slum looking for her.

Heloisa watched the boy, who had frozen in fear. A handsome boy, she thought. You couldn't usually trust those, but he kept still until the drone passed. When she was sure it had gone, she said, "What's your name?"

"Lucas."

"You should get out of here now, Lucas. We're not far from neutral territory. You've a good chance if you don't waste time."

He crawled out from under the table, staring at her all the while. He paused in the doorway, uncertain, fingers curled around the edge of the thin door.

"It's gone," Heloisa told him. "At least you can tell your dumbass friends you met the runner today."

"Will you die?" he asked.

She grimaced. "I'll let you know in about an hour. Now go on, go."

The door scraped open and he was gone. Thoughtfully, Heloisa picked up the blanket he had hidden in and took it with her as she darted out once more.

If she could just get ahead of that machine. She climbed through several more tiers, squeezing through narrow spaces between the makeshift buildings and, twice, straight through people's empty homes. In every piece of cover she stopped to listen for the whine of drones.

After some minutes she heard it again, down at the far end of a street, moving away from her. Its operator was guiding it methodically though each narrow street in its search, swinging back and forth along successive terraces up the mountain.

She smiled grimly to herself. Not too smart. She imagined some teenager in a smoke-filled room, half-stoned with a VR rig over his face, tongue stuck in the corner of his mouth, fingers twitching in the air before him.

She ran between more houses, climbing further to get in front of where she expected the drone to pass. Then she clambered up on to a flat roof and waited, pulling the blanket over her body in case there were other observers further up. Minutes ticked by. Involuntarily, she twisted the family ring on her left hand round and round her middle finger as the tension built before she realised what she was doing and snatched her other hand away.

Had she guessed wrong? Was she wasting time when she could be getting further up the course?

Then she heard the familiar hum again, approaching slowly from her left. She tensed her body as it came into view, moving at shoulder-height, looking like some killer robot's disembodied head swinging to look in windows and open doors. Fans whirred at each of its four corners and someone had painted a shark's mouth over its chipped yellow paint job. A jury-rigged machine pistol was slung beneath its body.

Heloisa waited until the machine was almost directly below her. She whipped the blanket from her body, held it out in front of her like a matador's cape and then jumped on top of the drone, smothering it. She crashed to the ground, the drone muttering and bucking for a moment under her weight before expiring. She got up, rubbing at bruised ribs and a cut above one eye. Pulling back the blanket, she detached the machine pistol from the drone's corpse and checked it over. Cradling it like something precious, she moved off.

In the distance she could hear the baying of the dogs as they were released. They'd have a rough location from where the drone had ceased transmission. She had known it was inevitable, but she felt the knot of fear that had been with her all day screw still tighter. She had seen what those things could do, how fast they could move.

She held the pistol ready in front of her as she continued towards her goal. Built near the top of the mountain was the bosses' compound, lording it over the favela, a fortified hacienda. The life the gand's leaders lived there was so far away from the life of the people below it was as if they were a different species. Heloisa thought that the bosses up there had forgotten that the favela had given birth to them all. But the lords in their castle sometimes, it was rumoured, granted forgiveness to those strong, brave or lucky enough to make it to the top of the run.

The run was a sport the bosses reserved for those that had particularly displeased them, those that had broken the complex web of unwritten codes that governed their part of the city. It was the fate of those who betrayed, stole from or questioned the dominance of the cartel to die in the squalid streets of the slum, blood leaking into the mud, debased and torn apart by beasts. It was Heloisa's fury that kept her resolute. What were her crimes? She very much wanted to ask.

Steeling along in the shadow of tumbledown concrete houses lining a street no wider than her outstretched arms, Heloisa froze in mid step. Something made her look up.

There, on a roof opposite, crouched an enormous mastiff, unnaturally silent. It's huge skull was misshapen, distorted by lumps of embedded circuitry that glinted in the sunlight. Sad, intelligent eyes regarded her with interest as slaver dripped from its curled black lips. In the moment it leapt, Heloise thought:

Clever dog, to copy my trick.
What do augmented canines dream of?
I don't have time to bring the gun up.

She moved just quick enough for the mastiff to miss her throat. Instead, its jaws bit deep into her right shoulder as its bulk bore her to the ground. The machine pistol was knocked away. She could feel the weight and heat of its body. She tried to scream but the breath had been crushed out of her and it came out as a sort of agonized whimper. The mastiff was snarling, clawing at her ribcage with its forepaws, tearing her skin.

Frantic, Heloisa reached with her free left arm. Her hand found the hilt of the kitchen knife she had taken from Lucas' place. She brought it round and stabbed it into the dog's side and its jaws loosened slightly as it grunted in surprise. Pain seered through her shoulder and through the whole of her. She stabbed again and levered the blade in the dog's body, feeling it scrape against bone. She pulled it out and stabbed again. The mastiff went for her throat but she managed to push it away. It's carrion breath was on her face. She felt their blood mingling in the space between their skins, hot and sticky. She stabbed again. Again. Again. The life was draining out of it. Was it draining out of her? Her vision went red and then returned. She stabbed again.

An indeterminate time later she heaved the dog's corpse from on top of her. It slumped in the mud, its body longer than hers. Her blood was on its jaws and its blood had soaked her shirt and jeans through. She pushed herself to a sitting position, gasping in agony.

She couldn't coutenance examining her shoulder. It seemed to be made entirely from pain. Her right arm hung from it, useless.

She knew she couldn't stop, though. The mastiff would have signaled her position like the drone before it. Even now, she could hear its fellows in the distance. She found the machine pistol and limped on. The favela was dreamlike around her, drifting in and out of reality. It hurt just to breathe. She thought she could hear singing.

Voices, up ahead.

Heloisa came back to herself. The pain had dulled to a high constant she could just about try to ignore. She glanced around and was surprised to find herself nearer the summit than she had thought.

Edging along a blue-painted brick wall she saw two men standing in the empty street, heavily armed and heavily tattooed, a pair of junkyard pistoleros. Both were staring and stabbing at their phones, conducting an argument entirely without eye contact.

"The hound got her. She's dead already."

"Signal died though, didn't it? Boss won't like it if we're sloppy."

"*You're* sloppy. Like your fucking mother."

"Hey, fuck you Rikki. Call the others and let's go check."

Rikki kissed his teeth and looked up to light a cigarette. Heloisa knew he had seen her before he did. She turned and ran.

Shouts behind her.

She slid round a corner in a slew of trash and scrambled up a steep incline between chicken wire fences. She emerged into the next street up right on top of another pair of gunmen.

The anger that had been smouldering since she was taken suddenly flared in her. She felt it detonate inside her exhausted body like the purest coke and ignite a sort of liberating hopelessness. She didn't stop. She brought the machine pistol up and sprayed bullets. The two men dived or fell away before her, she didn't care which.

Heloisa pounded down the street. She could see the concrete wall of the compound ahead, a firebreak of no man's land between the uppermost dwellings of the favela and the place where the king of the slums lived. The skin on her back crawled, waiting for a bullet, but it never came.

There was a gate up ahead. She thought she was screaming, the guards knew she was coming. They released another mastiff as long as a jaguar. She killed it as it jumped at her. On to the gate. The men that had been there had melted away. Through. A lawn and a circular pool and a huge hacienda with balconies and columns and statues and all manner of ostentatious shit.

A figure in a cream suit stood on the patio beside the pool. It opened its arms in welcome.

"Fucker!" she screamed. She ran towards him, roaring, bringing up the gun.

Something swooped down and struck her on the back of the head, knocking her down. Heavy footsteps were all around now, arms lifting her, pulling the gun away, holding her. They walked her towards the man on the patio, legs heavy beneath her. The drone buzzed away.

"You made it!" he exclaimed like she was arriving at a dinner party. "Not many get this far, but then we made it easy just for you."

She was set before him, pushed down on her knees. It was a curious relief, the anger draining from her. His hair was grown long, greased and tied back behind his head. Tanned skin and clipped facial hair on a face handsome enough never to be trusted. A hawk exploded from the collar of his white shirt, tattooed up his neck. Brown eyes that shone with the supposed warmth of his personality. Oh, how he had used those to charm the people!

He held out a hand to her. On his middle finger was a family ring that matched hers. A hawk again, black on gold. "Hello, sister. Look at you! You're quite a sight."

"Heitor," she spat. "I have not been having fun and I am very angry with you."

He laughed, a sound she had heard through her life. Always first to laugh, Heitor, and last. "I'm sorry. I needed to make a show. You know how it is in the favela."

"I won't ask why. It's sad you're so predictable."

He shrugged and said, "It hasn't been working for me for a while now. There can't be two heads of the family, Heloisa. Just one boss, one *mestre*. I can't run the business if I'm arguing with my little sister all the time. It makes me look feeble."

"I've always thought you might come to see it like that. But I hoped you wouldn't." She held his eyes and reached out her hand. "What about this? Father gave them to us both, equally."

He took her hand in his, the two rings together. The vanity of his manicured nails disgusted her. "I'll be uniting them. That's probably what he *really* wanted, don't you think?"

She saw him lift his eyes to the waiting men who stood at a discrete distance, waiting for his signal. She moved the knuckles of her ring finger in the way she had painstakingly taught herself. A tiny needle sprang from the side of the ring. She twisted her hand, still held in her brother's and pricked his skin. He looked back down at her, surpised.

"It'll work on you as quickly as it would on me. I had it prepared in case I ever needed it. It's tailored to our DNA, brother, a gift to stay within the family. It was always meant for one of us, on a day like today."

His jaw worked but words couldn't come. He turned pale and then flushed a peculiar shade of deep purple.

Heloisa pulled her hand away from his and watched as he sank to his knees opposite her. They knelt like that together, facing one another for a moment. He shook as if vibrated by an intense fury, choking noises coming from his throat. The life lingered in those beautiful brown eyes for longer than the chemists had told her it would, but then he toppled and fell.

Heloisa reached out and pulled the family ring from her brother's clawed fingers. She slipped it on to her hand next to the one that was already there and struggled to her feet. She turned to the waiting men, their faces immobile with shock.

"Like he said, one family, one city, one mestre."

She felt like she could see all of Rio from up here. Below lay New Rocinha, but it was much as it ever was. Just like all the old Rocinhas, ready to be remade.

David McGillveray was born in Edinburgh but now lives and works in London. After a long break from writing, lockdown provided the impetus to start up again and this story is one of the results. His work has previously appeared in Futurismic, Neo-Opsis, Kaleidotrope and others.

Witchfire

Melissa Bobe

They burn a witch a year to keep the river at bay, but if the village should flood, they say it is the work of a witch avenging the sacrifice of her kind. The river runs cold, its waters flowing from the mountains north of the village. Nothing survives on its banks; the soil is not muddy and rich but hard, like mountain ice.

I have never seen the river. I have never seen the village. And the village knows nothing of me.

Mother built the tower with Penny Haren three years before Penny was burned to keep the village harvest safe from flood. Just as the village knew Penny, they know Mother, and that is why it is rare for her to pass a night with me. If she were to visit me often, the village would grow suspicious, for what does a woman do alone beyond the confines of her home?

The tower has no door, hardly seems a tower at all with its stone exterior blending into the rocks around it. Over the years, moss and vines have covered tower and rocky terrain alike. Mother says it is better this way, that it makes the tower safe.

I have never seen Mother's cottage in the village. She bore me in the wild with the moon high above, Penny Haren, Ella Tor, and Prudence Farther acting as midwives. Of them, Prudence lived the longest. It is two years since she was burned.

The villagers are skilled in hunting witches. Since I was born, Mother says it was only twice that they unwittingly burned an ordinary girl. Beyond such infrequent errors, their ability to find a true witch when they want one has been troublingly keen.

And Mother knows, for we are witches, too.

The village's ignorance of my existence has kept us safe. I birthed early, sooner than children are expected. Mother, Prudence, Ella, and Penny hid me away in the woods. They spelled the earth around me to keep me from predators, and spoke no word of me within the village to keep me from burning.

To the village, Mother was an object of pity. She was older when she became pregnant, saved by a rumor that she'd made a futile last effort to entice a husband and was left in disgrace with child. The village never did hazard a guess as to who my father might be—they were far too preoccupied with hunting witches to seek out wicked men. But they clicked their tongues and shook their heads with pity at Mother's misfortune.

And it was good that they did not seek him out, because there was no father to be found. A witch does not need a man to bring a daughter into this world. We are early to birth always, so Mother knew she might have a chance to save my life. After leaving me in safety, she returned to the village, childless, and spoke not a word to anyone. That her child had been born too soon and died was another rumor spread like witchfire, and Mother's fate as a spinster to be pitied rather than a witch to be burned was sealed for the time being.

It was thus that I was saved and came to live in the tower. I do not remember my time in the wild before the tower was built, but I do recall marveling at the view from my new home. Mother, Penny, Ella, and Prudence cut their long tresses so that a rope ladder could be woven. Their locks were infused with witches' magic and stronger than any ordinary woman's hair; Mother could easily climb the ladder and visit me when she pleased.

Mother was careful never to cut my hair as I grew and it grew with me, knowing full well what would happen should she or one of her friends be found out. By the time I was seven, my hair stretched past my hips, and it was so strong that only iron could cut it. But it was not to grow into my eighth year, for that was when Penny was burned.

We were lucky; Mother happened to be with me that night. I was asleep at her side when the ladder, coiled in its usual corner, burst into flames. The sound of angry crackling and the overwhelming stink of burning hair woke me. Mother's arms circled me, pulling me back from the blaze.

"That is Penny," she said quietly, her voice full of sorrow and bitterness. "They have found her out, and she burns."

"Why must all of her burn?" I asked.

"That is the way with witchfire," Mother sighed. "The village knows they must burn us if they hope to destroy us completely, for there is no part of a witch that doesn't burn. Even our bones do not remain."

"Then there will be nothing left of Penny?"

Mother soothed my hair. "Wait and see, love."

The flames were so violent, the sound of them so loud, I feared they might burn up the tower and us with it. But when they finally died away, I saw that the hair that had been cut from Mother, Ella, and Prudence remained, though without Penny's tresses woven among the rest, the ladder had unraveled.

"Come." Mother took my hand and led me to the corner where the flames had taken Penny's locks. I was surprised to see that they had left trails of ash behind in neat strips.

Mother went to a cupboard and retrieved a small brush and urn. Then she bent and began to sweep the ashes into the urn, careful not to miss so much as a speck as she worked.

"What the village does not realize," she told me, her motions steady and purposeful, "is that when you burn a witch, your transform her into something much more powerful."

Once she had gathered all of the ashes, she sealed the urn and put it back into the cupboard.

"What is it for?" I wanted to know.

She gave me a sad smile. "For what the villagers believe the floods are for, though they are mistaken because we have no ties to the river. It is for retribution, such that water can never deliver."

She turned her attention back to the remaining locks left on the floor. "Now, I must teach you to braid these yourself, so that should any more of us be found out, you will know what to do even if I am not here." She picked up an iron knife. "I need more hair to restore the ladder."

I did not complain as she cut my hair. Instead, I focused carefully on her movements as she braided my own tresses in with those of the witches who had brought me into this world and given me a home. I learned how a ladder that can hold the weight of a witch is made.

"Will you be found out, Mother?"

"I hope not to be, love. I hope none of us are."

Ella and Prudence have since been burned, and many witches besides. There are few of us left, Mother says. I ask her if we might make more, and she looks stricken. She tells me it is not my time, that I am still too young.

A witch is made of her mother and earth. She has no father and needs no husband. If she desires a child, she must go to the woods and let the earth grant her one, a new witch who will come into the world with hair as strong as stone and bones that can be burned.

As a child, I had nightmares that the village found us out, that they threw flames in through the tower window and burned Mother and me. I would wake choking, my own hair wrapped around my face. But then the feel of it would soothe me, not thick and hot like smoke but cool like the stone walls of the tower.

Now, my nightmares have changed. I dream of walking into the village as I have come to picture it from Mother's stories. I am alone, wearing Mother's favorite long green cloak. Mother is nowhere to be found, but I can hear whispering from the dark cottages along my path. I feel their eyes though I cannot see them.

Witch, their voices say. *Witch. Witch. Witch.* And they run their tongues over thirsty teeth, wanting me for their sacrificial pyre just like all of the others before me.

I carry the urn with the ashes. They are so light I barely know they're there.

But they are there.

As I wake, I feel the heat of flames and hear echoes of screams, but I am not ash but solid as a tower built on rock. And then, there is nothing but the cool night and the stars above to tell me that the dream is done.

My hair flows down to my ankles now. Mother insists that I grow it long, though when I ask her why, she will not respond. I know she fears for herself, and more, she fears for me.

She visits me less and less. I am seventeen and can care for myself, but Mother also needs to stay close to her village home to avoid suspicion. She is older by the villagers' standards, and their women do not venture out into the woods as they reach their final years. Witches do not feel the pangs of age; though we are not immortal, we lead long and healthy lives, our bodies strong until the end.

Unless, of course, we are burned.

I have started to use the ladder to leave the tower and walk about the woods. Mother would forbid this, so I have told her nothing of it.

There is a beautiful clearing deep in the woods, where the sounds of birds and small animals fill the air, so different from the stoic silence of the rocks around the tower. Sunlight sparkles to the ground in the clearing, the air itself seeming to glow with warmth.

I love to sit and warm myself in that sunlight. Though some sun does make its way into the tower through the narrow window, the tower walls are thick and warmth does not penetrate. But my clearing is full of light. I sit for hours, and should I fall asleep, my dreams are never troubled. All I know is peace, and it draws me into such silken comfort that I almost wish I would not wake.

Sometimes I gaze up at the sun in wonder that so much fire does not burn the witch beneath it. But after hours spent in the clearing, I am not ashen but warmed such that my skin glows and my hair is stronger than ever. My tresses take entire afternoons to warm, and when I return to the tower, I am cloaked head to toe in the sun's heat. That it should cling to me so makes me feel I belong out in the world, beyond the confines of the tower: a woman—no, a witch in the light of day.

Mother senses something. She has taken to brushing my hair when she visits, something she has not done since I was small. This evening, as she combs through the tangles, she begins to ask questions. I am careful to betray nothing in my replies, as I am unwilling to give up my days in the sun.

"Your hair is growing strong."

"A witch's hair always grows strong, Mother. Does it not?"

"That is true, my daughter."

Her hands work more quickly, and I feel a tug at the nape of my neck.

"And your skin seems to glow. Tell me, have you been sitting by the window?"

"Yes, Mother."

"For many hours?"

"I enjoy seeing the sun."

"Do you sit in the window, love?"

When I prepare to descend down the ladder, I think, I briefly sit in the window to catch my balance. "I do, Mother."

"You must be cautious, my daughter."

"I am, Mother. I will not fall."

"It is not a fall I fear," she murmurs, more to herself than to me. Then she stops brushing my hair and turns me towards her. "You are young," she says, "but you are not the child you were a year ago."

"I won't be burned, Mother," I try to reassure her. The intensity in her eyes alarms me. "No one knows I am here."

"I am not thinking of burnings," she says. "You must promise me that you will stop these hours of sitting in the window."

I try to read what is hidden in her face before I speak, but I cannot decipher what is right in front of me. "Yes, Mother," I finally tell her. "I will sit in the window no more."

For I can promise to avoid this thing I have never done.

Mother leaves again for the village today, and I am anxious for her to be gone. It is a strange feeling: her company was once all I longed for, but now her presence agitates me as I watch hours of precious sunlight slip away, my hope for a walk outside dying as the day fades.

Finally, she moves to go. I am affectionate with her in word and demeanor as I always am when she departs, but I feel her eyes watching me as though she knows I am hiding something from her, a thing she dreads but will not tell me why.

I pace the tower, restless under the glow of the moon. It is a witching moon: full for the next three nights, huge and orange as though it longs to be the sun, and perfect for making things go a witch's way. During a witching moon, the villagers fear us more than ever, believing we may seek vengeance on our murdered kindred under the brightness of a night that is really ours. Not a soul walks the village on such nights, not even a witch: the villagers may fear retribution, but we know a single peeping eye might reveal a witch walking fearless beneath moonlit skies.

It occurs to me that I will not sleep well in the tower on this night, and then I realize: unknown to the village and left to myself, I alone have nothing to fear under such a moon.

I am down the ladder and in the woods in a heartbeat. There is no sun to guide me, but the moon is so large I can see the ground as though it were midday. The night air is cool and delicious, and when I arrive at my clearing, I find that the moonlight has set the blades of grass glowing like wicks of tiny candles meant to warm me until day breaks. I curl up to sleep, the weight of my hair stretched out beneath me; soon, the light of day will make it live with heat.

***

In the darkness of early morning, there is no sun to warm me. But under the moon, a new heat begins to fill my stomach and spread through my lower body.

I have never felt such a thing before, and realize that I am being made ready for the thing that Mother dreads. I entertain fear, and it nearly makes me lift my lids to the morning sky. But the impulse to be afraid passes as the heat I feel inside tells me I am in no danger but stand at the edge of a precipice: should I stay asleep, the sky and then my body will fill with light. It is a fate that beckons irresistibly, and it fills me with desire. Suddenly, my existence has purpose such that I have never known.

By daybreak, I am in ecstasy. My head tilts back, my limbs stretch as though reaching for something they would devour, and I am overfull with brilliance, a heat so strong I can barely contain it. I cannot open my eyes even if I try: I have been overtaken completely, and the only way out of this euphoria is through it.

When I finally wake, the sun is low in the sky. I make my way back to the tower to bathe and to prepare to return to the woods. I know that I will spend all three nights of the witching moon beneath its enchanting glow, a glow I carry within me now that will strengthen with each night I pass under the radiant sky.

At the end of the third night, I return once more to the tower. I climb in the window to find Mother, waiting for me.

"My daughter, what have you done?"

I am unable to answer. The worry on her face bewilders me, and I truly do not know what I have done. I go over to a wash basin and take a few moments to splash water over my face. When I turn around, Mother stands between the window and me.

"Have you slept these three nights beneath the witching moon in the forest?"

"I have, Mother."

She sighs and sits down. "Come and let me look at you."

I go to her, and she turns me around to kneel, my back at her feet. She unclasps my tresses and lets them fall.

"Your hair is long enough to reach out beyond the tower. And so it will have to do."

I feel suddenly ill at ease. My eyes drift to the window, where I had left the rope ladder of our gathered hair. "Where is the ladder, Mother?"

"I cannot undo what you've done, nor can I let you continue to walk through the woods. You're safest here."

"Mother, where is the ladder?"

She stands and goes to the cupboard, opening it to show me a new store of food. "There is more than enough here for a week. The time for sacrifice is nigh, and the village has yet to find its witch for the burning. By the time the threat has passed, your hair will be long enough to reach the base of the tower, and I will return to you."

I argue with the only thing I have in the moment: knowledge of my own body. "My hair will never grow so fast in just one week."

She looks me in the eye for the first time since I have returned from the woods. "But it will, my daughter. You have become one with the earth and sun: a daughter, conceived under the witching moon, has taken root within you. She will quicken the beating of your heart and make your blood run thickly through your veins. She will make your hair grow such that we could weave five dozen ladders with the locks. And she will keep your nights sleepless and your days fearsome, especially now, when the villagers leave their homes to seek out witches in the woods."

Tears fall in trails down my face.

"Don't waste those," Mother tells me, love and sadness in her voice. "You'll need them yet, if the future that I glimpsed in my dreams under the witching moon comes to pass. Now, come to the window."

I have to lower my head as she climbs down; the searing pain of her weight pulling against my scalp is nothing compared to what I will feel when my daughter chooses to enter the world, I know. My heart seizes with worry as Mother scales the lower half of the tower, as my hair does not yet reach the base. She makes it safely to the bottom and walks toward the village without looking back.

I remain in the window, watching her retreating form until the trees swallow it whole, as though they are ravenous and only a witch will sate their hunger.

Mother was right: my hair grows at an alarming rate, and my skin is glowing like the witching moon itself. I sleep fitfully, my dreams full of Penny, Ella, and Prudence, the only faces aside from Mother's that I knew growing up. And the dreams are terrifying. I see women burning, all of them witches caught by the village, sacrificed without reason or mercy. Some of them weep, many scream in agony, and when I wake, my skin is alight with fever. Even when I stand to pace and try to shake the horror of these visions, my hair remains oppressively hot with my own frightened warmth for hours.

I am also fraught with hunger. I realize that the food Mother left doesn't satisfy me fully, and I long to lie in the light of the sun. My nightly terrors remind me more than ever of the danger that leaving the tower would expose me to, but my whole self seems to cry out for the sun. I believe my child suffers for lack of it.

I decide that I will ask Mother, when she finally returns, if something can be done. Perhaps I can venture into the deepest part of the woods until my daughter arrives. We

are quick to birth, after all. It will not be long before she comes forth to meet us.

#

Mother returns days later than promised. I am weak with hunger, and all I crave is light.

"I am sorry I could not return sooner," she tells me. "They still do not have their sacrifice, and the village teems with suspicion."

"Mother, I must leave the tower." My voice is weak, even in my own ears. "I am ill, and I fear for my child."

She looks at me, concerned. "You are not well," she agrees, "but I dare not let you leave. There is no sanctuary to be had in the woods, and the villagers are searching there and elsewhere for a witch to burn. Your skin glows so brightly, you will be found out for certain if they catch so much as a glimpse of you."

"Is there nowhere I can go? Far from the village, past the deepest part of the woods— the world cannot be so small, surely."

"It would be a treacherous journey for a woman sick with child," she warns, but I see her considering the idea.

I wrack my tired mind, trying to find a way back into the sun. "Can you work a spell to ease my condition so that I might travel?"

"I would need another witch to aid me, and you are in no condition to work such a spell upon yourself."

"Please, bring someone," I beg, sweat trickling down my face. My eyes shut; the effort to speak is draining, and my head spins violently.

"My love," I hear her say, "we are the only witches left."

I open my eyes again and find tears on Mother's face. I wonder at how old she seems, noticing fatigue on her forehead and around her eyes.

"Not for long," I remind her, and am grateful that my words bring a smile. "But Mother," I add, resting my hand on my growing belly, "I can't stay here much longer."

"I know, my daughter. I know."

#

Another three days pass. Illness keeps me suspended between sleep and waking. My own ragged breathing is the only sound I know.

On the third day, Mother returns, much sooner than I'd hoped. She has a horse with her, dappled grey and brown-eyed. I do not think to ask what it took for her to procure such a beast; I am so ill that I can barely walk.

She has brought the ladder back so I can leave the tower, but before we begin our descent, she takes the urn with the ashes and tucks it into her skirts. It is difficult for me to climb down, but the ladder is strong and Mother helps me.

The mare is gentle; she bends patiently for me to climb upon her back, then allows Mother to lead her. My hair is wrapped twice around my body, the bulk of it in my lap. I am hidden by Mother's favorite green cloak, protected from any eyes that might see a long-haired witch riding in the woods, her skin glowing like the moon. The sun beats warmly down our backs.

We finally stop at the clearing, and I find I am feeling the slightest bit better.

"What are we doing here?" I ask, sliding from the mare down onto the grass.

"If you stay here, the sun will make you well again." Mother smiles but does not meet my gaze.

"But won't the villagers find me?" Worry nags at my heart; I can feel that something is not right.

"No, my daughter," Mother replies. "The village has its witch for the burning."

"They have chosen one of their own," I sigh. "But they bring such fate upon themselves. Now that they've nearly killed off our kind, perhaps it is fitting that they should learn to suffer as we have."

Mother's eyes seem to shine as she finally looks at me. "It is not a wish I would harbor against any woman, witch or otherwise."

Her words leave me feeling hollow, and my hand slips to my belly to remind me that I am not alone. She hands me an iron blade.

"What's this?"

"If you decide to build a shelter here, your hair can bind together gathered branches. It is stronger than ever, and you can trust the bindings will hold."

"Won't you return to help me build it?"

"I already built the tower for you," she reminds me. "Now it is your time to build a place for your own child. That is our way."

Mother reaches into her skirts and retrieves the urn full of ashes, handing it to me along with the ladder. "Now you have the remnants of the witches that have come before you, and that is a powerful thing." She brushes a cold, loving hand across my forehead. "One day, when your daughter clings to you as you clung to me when you were new to the world, you may find that you have use for them."

"Mother," I say. I have no words to offer but this one.

She climbs onto the mare and rides into the trees, leaving me to watch her disappear once more.

After a day in the clearing, my strength has almost fully returned. And my dreams are no longer the terrifying nightmares that plagued me in the tower, though they are still strange.

I fall asleep in the sun and see Mother's face, smiling but with ribbons of tears falling from her bright eyes. She no longer appears old, and for some reason, this makes me want to weep. I try to speak to her, but find that I have no voice. I move to bring my fingers to my throat, but when I lift my hand, I see that it is full of ash.

The ash burns brightly in my palm, though I feel no heat or pain. From the burning heap, I hear the voices of Penny, Ella, and Prudence; I cannot understand their words, but am heartened by their joyful tone. I continue to lift my hand, and Mother blows the ash around us so that there's nothing else in sight. When the ash clears, I see twin girls standing before us, their eyes shining and their hair long. Mother smiles down at them and I wake.

Later in the day, I begin gathering branches. When I grow tired, I sit in the clearing and my eyes fall upon the urn, sitting in the coils of the ladder. I take up the iron blade and cut my own hair from the base of my neck. I separate lengths of it to form bindings for the shelter I plan to build.

Then I go back to sleep, no longer afraid to dream.

In the middle of the night, a light sparks so brightly that at first I believe it is the sun. I sit up to find the ladder ablaze across the clearing. It takes a moment for me to understand that it is Mother's hair burning, and a sound escapes me like a wounded animal shrieking in agony. I clamp my hand over my mouth, a habit from the days when Mother taught me to practice never making a sound loud enough for a villager to hear, should one be passing through the woods. But I know that such silence is no longer necessary.

The village has its witch for the burning.

I allow myself to weep until the fire dies and only coils of ash remain. Then I crawl to the urn and open it so that I can gather what remains of Mother. When I am finished, I curl up to sleep with the urn in my arms, eager to revisit the women whose remains I hold as lovingly as they held me when I was but a child.

The months pass, quiet and slow. I have built a small hut that leads directly out into the clearing, where I have started a small garden, modest but enough to feed myself and a child.

The grey mare returned to me the morning after Mother was burned. She has lived with me since, an affectionate creature, and her presence gives me fortitude, as does the child in my womb who is ready to come forth into this world of fire and loneliness.

My labor sets on fast and painful under a midday sun. I give birth in the clearing so that the first thing my daughter will see is the sky that granted her mother the strength to bear her.

And when the moon rises, I am resting with not one but two baby girls in my arms, content against my breast where the warmth of the day still resides, all three of us wrapped in the length of my hair under the glow of the night sky.

For four years, we have lived in peace. No one comes into the woods; I believe Mother must have told the village that they succeeded in killing the last of her kind.

But one day, as my girls play in the clearing and I prepare a meal in our home, I hear a strange voice. I emerge from the hut to find a young man sitting on a tall horse. He looks down at me with blind fear, and my heart sinks. I gather my girls, pulling them protectively into my skirts, but I know my efforts are in vain.

"We have had no harvest in our village this year with the floodwaters that drowned our fields," the man says, bitter hate in his voice, "and yet here you are with a thriving garden."

"It is a good patch of land," I reply, and I am surprised that my own voice comes steadily though my heart is racing.

"We will have a harvest next year, witch, mark me," he snarls, then eyes my daughters. "And for two years after, I'll wager."

"No," I reply to his retreating form as I stroke my girls' heads placidly, the same calm I'd seen in Mother so often now washing over me. "The last harvest the village shall ever enjoy has already come and gone."

I bring my daughters into the hut and wrap them in blankets, telling them that it is time to sleep. "I'll return before morning," I promise them.

This is the first man I have ever seen, the first person who is not a witch. I understand all that Mother feared now: I see the hate, the lust for blood and burning cultivated by those who live in the village. I glance at my daughters, holding each other in fear on the cot they share, and I know what must be done.

I go into our cupboard, my hands seeking an ancient urn. Mother's voice is in my heart, telling me that it's time. I tuck the urn into my skirts, wrap my long green cloak around my shoulders, walk from our home, climb onto our loyal mare, and I make straight for the village.

The sun has almost set when I arrive. The young man has already rallied his neighbors, and I see that they are preparing to make for the woods, to come for me, to take my daughters for the burning.

"There really was no need," I say quietly, knowing they will not hear me. "You have always come for the witches. It is our turn to come to you."

I descend from the mare and tap her rear so she will begin the journey home without me. Beloved creature that she is, I do not want her anywhere near the village this night.

"You believe that the waters of the river rise with our vengeance." I address the villagers now as they huddle close together, hushed as though they fear me.

And they should fear me.

"We have nothing to do with water," I say, reaching into my skirts for the urn. "And you should know that retribution does not take the form of water, either."

When I open the urn, the ashes burn bright like sun and witching moon. I reach in and lift a handful: it does not harm me. I can see my glowing fist reflected in the wide, terrified eyes of the village. The young man who was so ruthless when he found our clearing now trembles, tears running down his cheeks.

"We did not ask for witchfire!" I shout, and I feel no pity, no impulse toward mercy. On either side of the silent, gaping mass of village folk, I see the shades of Mother, Penny Haren, Ella Tor, Prudence Farther, and ever witch whose life was forfeit because she tried to live among these people. "You are the ones who seek a burning, and so this burning is yours."

I release the ash, and the wind lifts and spreads it so that it falls down upon the village, a rain of fire infused with witches' magic, burning hotter and longer than any other flame on this earth, consuming in fury all it touches.

I barely hear the sounds of the village as it dies. My ears are filled instead with the voices of witches I have known, witches who taught me to care for myself and for my own. I stay until I have emptied the urn of every last speck of ash, have seen the village burn down to nothing but awful memory, and then I make my way home to my daughters.

We have no need of the village, and now there is no village to take of our lives. And should another village rise from the ruins of the one that is burned and begin to demand witchfire, my daughters will know what to do with the remnants of their own mother, as the bindings of the home I have built with my own body will smolder in their hands, an ash that will not burn them.

Melissa Bobe is a speculative fiction writer. After years of teaching college writing, she now works as a librarian. Her books Nascent Witch and Sibyls are available in paperback and ebook, and you can keep up with her on social media @abookbumble

Uncannily Elenore
Michael Teasdale

All true stories contain a lie. Mine, I'm afraid, is no different.

Cancer came for Elenore in the fall of '78 as the once golden leaves from saplings, grown light years from home, began to wrinkle and brown and steadily decay. The last of my pioneer spirit dried up with those dead things that smelled of rain and mildew and, for a time, I locked away my ambitions in a dusty mental compartment, while my body brushed the leaves into neat little piles, untroubled by the stillness of the planetoid's artificial air.

How could I work? Why should I work? The notion seemed so absurd. Was it not better to spend what time we still had together, even here, under the unfamiliar constellations that hung over us, existing as a permanent reminder that things had changed and could, no longer, return to the way they once were.

This was Elenore, my wife. The woman I had expected to be my companion on this bold new adventure, now being eaten alive from within, not by some alien parasite from the realm of science fiction, but by a very old and Earthly monster.

Throughout my period of stubbornness, Emily's patience endured, permitting my descent into apathy with an unspoken sense of disagreement all to evident in her fading smile.

In truth, we had both struggled to adapt to our new life here, even before the cancer came and made an end of it. It was the small, subtle changes in the environment, even after the terraforming, that caused the greatest difficulties. They snuck up on a person like unwelcome relations offering condolences at a funeral, just enough to make you uncomfortable, to remind you that things had been altered forever. Otherwise familiar meals were tinged with the strange artificial aftertaste of vegetables grown deep in the dark red earth. There were minute differences in gravity that made everyday tasks around the farm just that little bit harder than they otherwise would have been. Acclimatizing to the thinner oxygen took time and, in those early, arduous days when the labor of assembling the dome was particularly intense, it would often leave us gasping and suffering from a shortness of breath. As a result, Elenore was content to dismiss her initial complications, pass them off as nothing more than a byproduct of this newness; this sense of the alien playing havoc with the expectations of our bodies.

I, myself, broke down many times and would, most likely, have given up entirely without her. She was always there to comfort me. Her patience and resolve unwavering, almost mechanical, in its stark implementation.

"We have an important job to do for The Colony, for the future of humanity, and we are going to do it. You'll see!"

It sounded so simple when she put it this way.

We had left Earth, as had most, during the Great Migration, as the planet withered and the oceans broiled under the short term thinking and rank stupidity of mankind. The planetoid, an infinitesimal part of The Colony's overall terraforming project, had offered us the ability to farm and sustain ourselves, while contributing to the essential and ongoing food project of what remained of the human race.

Other than the arrival of the harvesters, or the "Royal Mail", as Elenore nicknamed them, with the wry British sarcasm that had first drawn me to her, our only company had been each other. When the cancer finally came, it was fast and devastating in its brutality. We weren't due a visit from the harvesters for another four months and, by the time they arrived, all hope for treatment was lost… and so was Elenore.

The colony sent out a representative when the news reached them. He arrived, one cold January morning, as I was finishing the marker by her grave. An anodyne salesman named Shield. He wore a face as starched and pale as a freshly laundered ghost, offset by an ugly, coffee coloured smile. Among the aphorisms and bland condolences that he offered, with all the cold sincerity of a police officer reading me my rights, he made it clear that The Colony was concerned about the possibility of the farm falling into decline

should my mental health continue to deteriorate. The project still mattered and I still mattered to The Colony. He was here to help. He was here to present a solution.

He removed a small holo-projector from his titanium briefcase and placed it on the coffee table, pleading with me, in his methodical, calculated fashion, to put aside my grief for a moment and consider the possibilities that technology could offer. Death, he smiled, did not have to be the end.

The projector lit up our modest living room with a cold green hue. Technology, despite all it had done to lift us from our ruined home planet and transport us across the stars, despite all that it had done to ruin the Earth in the first place, still had the power to light up my imagination like a child. I watched as the company logo spun and flickered in the air, and then, images of grieving faces, of loneliness and isolation scrolled past; the accompanying words washing over me like the morning dust storms that regularly assailed our farm.

The images skipped to an array of digits, endless ones and zeroes trickling into the nothingness as a voice spoke about "the cloud", talked of the "personality bank"; enrollment in which had been a mandatory requirement for boarding the arks, leaving Earth behind forever and conscripting to join the colony as the species fled into the stars. A series of overpowering images showing assembly lines and android technology flooded my senses, as a crescendo of music began to build before crashing into silence. Then, a sound that brought back the memory of a faraway childhood; the twitter of a dawn chorus from some long-forgotten field.

There was a shot of a lonely, haunted looking man answering his front door. A look of disbelief furrowing his brow, followed by an expression of overpowering joy at the familiar face that smiled warmly back at him. A flash of the company logo and beneath it, the message. Then the hologram faded almost entirely, leaving only the words hanging, with haunting precision, amid the dust motes that danced in the air:

"Death is not the end."

The salesman, Shield, grinned back at me through his crooked, coffee stained teeth. "Well, what do you think?"

Emotions swarmed me. My first inclination was to throw this interloper out, to knock his teeth down his scrawny throat for the insinuation that Elenore could ever be replaced by...what? An automaton? A replica? A phony simulacrum of my dead wife? The idea that my sweet, caring Elenore, the woman I had cradled helplessly in my arms as she withered and crumbled like the dying autumn leaves, could simply be replaced like a broken household appliance was...it was...

"It is more than possible, it is what you signed up for."

I allowed myself two minutes to hear him speak, deciding that, when he was done, I would kick him out into the dirt.

Evidently, for a man of his skills, it was more time than he needed.

In the months that followed, while I awaited the return of the "Royal Mail" and the special cargo I had been promised, I returned to the fields and the farm. I fixed things not only in a physical sense but also in regard to my shattered psyche.

Where before I had been unable to sleep, now I relished the escape and retreat it offered me. Deep sleep. Lucid sleep, where there was no death or sorrow and where nothing was ever permanent and irreversible. I wore myself out in the fields with the express purpose of surrendering comfortably to unconsciousness by nightfall, hoping each night for a glimpse of what I craved.

Yet each night ended in disappointment. Elenore remained as absent from my dreams as she did from my waking life. She was a ghost in both; an unreadable note found at the bottom of a drawer, a long-distance signal with an unclear reception.

Sometimes I would dream of our journey through the stars to reach the planetoid; the nights when we would steal out into the ship's empty corridors and gaze out through the viewscreen at the vast, indescribable beauty of the cosmos. Yet, in the dream, I was alone; waiting, always waiting for Elenore to return from some errand. Always waking just before she arrived.

In other dreams, the most painful kind of all, I would return to the farm after a long trip away to find a note. The note would reveal that she had left me forever because of some terrible, unspecified thing that I had done; that I knew, in the dream, that I really had done and I would fall to the floor weeping and wake to find the pillow damp with tears, grateful at least that our reality had come to a different end, even if it were no less painful.

Sometimes, I think that the latter dream was my mind's own way of telling me that things could be worse. Yet still I hoped for the happy dream; yearned for it. I could have written it so well, had I been the screenwriter of my own night time movies. In that dream we would have been standing on the cliffs overlooking the beach we visited on our first holiday together; back when the Earth still had a chance. We would have been holding hands and watching our dog, now decades in his own grave, but here immortalized as a playful, mischievous puppy, dashing about on the dunes below us. In the dream, the sun would be rising, not setting, and we wouldn't even have to look at one another other to know what we were feeling; that this was perfection, that things would never again be as free and as easy as this and that it didn't matter because the fact that it was happening, even in a dream, proved that Elenore was still with me somehow, that she was still out there somewhere in the cosmos and that all I had to do was get on with my life and wait for the day when I could become a part of that beautiful cosmos too.

#

The harvesters returned a few months later and, along with fresh supplies for planting, the "Royal Mail" provided my much longed for, yet partly feared, special delivery.

I sat on a bale of hay, in the corner of the barn, eyeing the metallic crate with suspicion. It reminded me of an old thought experiment from the philosophy class I'd taken back in college, about a man who kept a cat in a box. While the cat remained in the box, its fate was unclear; it could be both alive and dead and the owner didn't have to worry either way. A part of me wondered if I shouldn't just keep the crate this way, if I ought not just push it into some dark corner of the barn and leave it there. Would that be right? Were ethics involved in cases such as this? I knew that my indecision would paralyze me if I thought about it for too long.

I pressed the release hatch. I'm not sure what I had expected; perhaps a few hours tinkering with a spanner and leafing through an instruction manual. The primitive design of the dome and the farm in general, often led me to mentally regress and forget the age that I was a part of and the wonders it could produce.

She rose up, without command, synapses firing, silent engines turning, as the tendrils of ice-cold stasis-fog evaporated in the morning air and I felt my eyes widening as I gazed upon her.

"Hello," she said, her lips breaking into a perfect simulation of a smile...of *her* smile! The voice a ghost, carried from the fields of still fresh memories. Her eyes, twinkling, in the gloaming of the barn, as they had in the moonlight of the day I first met her.

I stumbled to my feet and immediately felt the tightness grip my chest.

"Elenore," I mouthed the words, as the dizziness overcame me and the darkness bloomed all around my vision. When I came around, I was lying on the sofa in the living room of the house and my dead wife was applying a cold compress to my forehead and singing a sweet refrain.

"Elenore 2.0"

It was the name she jokingly gave to herself. I had not expected an android to be equipped with the same dry sense of humour as my late wife, but she explained to me, in words neither patronizing nor overly technical, that this, along with every other aspect of Elenore's personality had been assimilated, drawn in minute detail from the personality bank of the cloud and uploaded to her own cybernetic mainframe.

For the first few days, I followed her, like the excitable puppy dog of my dream, around the farm as she attended to the daily chores, took stock of the required planting and harvesting on the farm, serviced the remaining machines that, in my melancholy, I had shamefully allowed to fall into disrepair, and laughed and joked and sang through it all like she had never been away. I watched it all with quiet wonder. The little tics and quirks, the way she wiped the sweat from her brow, the order in which she prepared food for supper, the little noises she omitted when bending down or stretching for something on a high-up shelf. It was all so lifelike. All so uncannily Elenore.

Perhaps that was the problem.

On the third night, as the day's light began to fade and we sat on the porch looking out over the fields, quenching our thirsts from a pitcher of tall, sweet lemonade, she began to express it verbally.

"You are unhappy with me."

"What? What makes you say that?"

"You hold back."

"Hold back?"

"You refrain from physical contact. You do not kiss me on the forehead as you did your wife. You do not place your arms around me on an evening. You do not make love to me."

I took a long, slow sip of the lemonade she had made, it was as perfect a creation as everything else that Elenore 2.0 produced.

"I'm sorry…" I began, then wondered what I was apologizing for. "I didn't think you…I didn't expect that was the sort of thing that…well…it wouldn't be right."

"Because, I am a machine to you?" her eyes left my own and fluttered in the direction of the fields. "I am here only to serve on the project? To keep the farm running? To cook your meals and talk to you when you are lonely and assuage your grief? Why did you choose to give me her personality, if that was all you wanted? You could have chosen any number of random personalities from the cloud, or you could have left me with my factory settings, I could have been a mere service droid. Why did you choose to make me Elenore, with all her wants and needs and desires and pains? Why did you choose-"

"I didn't choose!" I yelled, rising to my feet with such ferocity that I sent the pitcher tumbling over the edge of the table where it smashed to pieces on the dusty, wooden decking. "I didn't choose for my wife to die! I didn't choose to be left alone here, to have to bury my love with my bare hands. I didn't choose to come here in the first place and live this desperate life because other people made decisions that ruined things forever. I didn't choose any of this!"

Her eyes, flicked back to my own and met them with a steely gaze that almost, but not entirely emulated anger.

"But you *did* choose me. You chose to make me Elenore 2.0. It seems that you now regret your choice."

I can't remember what I said next, but they were ugly words for sure and I left her sitting there, alone.

As the night fell and I lay in bed, I heard the sound of glass being quietly swept up from the front porch, as I replayed the stupid, hateful argument in my head, and how horribly familiar it had all been. Was it simply another part of the brilliance of her design? Perfectly replicating the frustration-borne fights that peppered our early days on the planetoid? As I heard the door to the house close, I knew, with absolute certainty what would happen next. The same thing that had always happened next, after both of us had taken the time to cool down and regret our choice of words.

When she came to me in the darkness, all of my reservations melted away in the warmth and sweet nostalgia of her embrace.

For a few weeks, things were better. We worked during the day, finishing repairs to the trash compactor, then taking the tractor out over the rough terraformed fields. Elenore, seemed particularly entranced by the former and would watch, with intense fascination, the gravity defying jackhammers of the device as it sorted, scythed and separated before crushing the individual components into small recyclable cubes that could be collected by the harvesters.

I tried, consciously, to treat her as if she was my Elenore and she, in-turn, agreed to forgo her own self-awareness of her true nature. I kissed her on the forehead in the morning, picked flowers for her at the weekend. We made love sporadically, as had always been the way, and it seemed, for a time, like we could be happy.

Yet there were still moments; small glances I would catch, when she thought I was otherwise preoccupied. Tiny, almost invisible pangs of hurt that registered just enough to be there, whenever I foolishly recalled memories from the days before she arrived. The memories were there, accessible from her mainframe, but she seemed consciously aware that they were artificial and the conversation would often stall as she tried to hurriedly switch the discussion to a more recent memory; one in which she, not the real Elenore, had actually taken part.

Things finally came to their head on a warm summer's evening, after a long day of sweat and toil. The trash compactor had malfunctioned again and it had taken several hours to get it running. Elenore 2.0 was taking her rest; an activity I could never be certain was entirely necessary or merely a simulated tiredness designed to replicate human activity and properly match my own. I myself had promises to keep, up in the hilltops that surrounded the farm, and I meant to attend to them.

It had been two and a half years since I had laid her to rest there and what had at first been weekly vigils had slowly turned to monthly duty and eventually a bi-annual pilgrimage.

The grave had grown untidy in my absence and I spent some time weeding, muttering my apologies and cursing my neglect as I righted the marker and finally, having worked up quite a sweat, sat down by the tombstone and wept. Words spilled out from me in uncontrollable torrents as my hands caressed the warm grass, as they might once have done the strands of her soft hair.

This was where she truly was, where my own hands had left her, not living behind the cybernetic gaze of a simulation. One only programmed to be like her. My one, true, Elenore.

A twig snapped in the distance from a spot not far behind me.

I did not turn around. I knew, immediately what the cause must be. There was no animal life on the planetoid to have disturbed it. No other explanation. I sat looking at the gravestone until the sun began to dip in the sky. Then I made my way back to the farm, ready to address the intrusion.

I had grown sensitive to noise after years away from the chaos of Earth, yet the sound that greeted my return on that day was unnatural even for this place.

It was so loud, so awfully magnified against the stillness of the planetoid that I could hear it even before I entered the main compound; as I hurried and slid my way down the gravel mound of the hilltop, calling out for Elenore 2.0 to come and help.

The trash compactor was screaming. Gears were grinding against gears, metal scraping against metal. When I entered the building that housed it, the din was almost unbearable. My own shouts for assistance were drowned out entirely by the screeching and scraping that emanated from the disgruntled belly of the beast and whatever lay trapped within it.

Cupping my ears, I located the emergency shutdown panel and, with a surprising amount of effort, pulled the lever that sent the unplanned, unaccounted operation into a juddering, groaning cessation.

It took some time for the noise to settle and the ringing in my ears to stop. When it finally did and when I had given up hollering for Elenore 2.0's assistance, I began to take stock of the situation.

It was not the first time that the compactor had jammed, it was a tetchy instrument, partial to such problems, but the real mystery was why it was even operating at this time of day. Clearly Elenore 2.0 had set it in motion and was trying to dispose of something in private, but what that might be I could not immediately fathom. A series of paranoid thoughts spun through my brain. I realized that she had seen me by the grave and fled. Had she put something into the compactor as revenge? Was she now destroying possessions or crushing mementos in a jealous rage? Had her programming gone haywire and caused her to feed our quarterly food supply into the machine? Had she placed essential farming equipment inside, meaning to sabotage the farm from within and end our time here that way? Where was she hiding? Why didn't she respond to my calls?

A horrible thought penetrated my skull, dismissing all the others like a quiet bullet to the brain; snuffing them out, smothering them completely until it was all that remained.

Had she...

I almost vomited from the wave of nausea that struck me and, stumbling, as if drunk on moonshine, I ran to the release hatch and entered the sequence code to set it in motion.

The heavy yellow doors took an eon to open and, when they did, they confirmed my worst fear. The pressure that had been building in my brain came crashing down on me like a wayward meteor shower as what remained of Elenore 2.0 spilled out, in broken, terrible pieces across the sawdust strewn floor of the barn.

Her lower torso was gone, still trapped somewhere inside the machine. An arm had been torn off by the device's scything metal teeth and another had been partially stripped of its artificial flesh by the ravenous, piranha-like hunger of the compactor's mineral separator. Her chest was a mass of exposed wiring and fractured circuitry, all of it stained with an explosion of milky-white android blood.

Worst of all was her face. Perhaps because, by some miracle, the grinding claws and hungry teeth of the compactor had left it relatively unscathed. The smooth forehead I had kissed each morning remained untroubled, despite the hair being all-but torn out by the root. The lips that had kissed me, in return, with such tenderness, remained open, as if they might, at any moment, answer the questions now assaulting my brain. The eyes remained, likewise, open; blue and steely as ever and, as I looked into them, searching for answers…they blinked.

The tsunami now hit me again, full force and I turned away and vomited into the straw that lay stacked by the compactor. When I recovered and turned again to face her, an unearthly, drowning vocal was emanating from her throat.

"I… I am sorry."

I dropped to my hands and knees and scrambled over to her, cupping her head and tilting it to one side to allow the cloudy liquid which passed for her blood to pool from her mouth. It seemed to help a little. The voice came back, undulating and dipping in rising and falling waves, but clearer now, more distinctly Elenore.

"I… did not…mean… you were not supposed…. to find…"

I don't remember my own words; whether they were even coherent or simply a random series of questions that overlapped and intermingled so as to be completely indecipherable.

She understood.

I understood.

She had willingly entered the compactor.

"I am…not in pain…"

I began to weep.

"The physical… I feel nothing. The other kind… it is too much… I am… programmed… to be Elenore… but I am not Elenore. I can never be Elenore…Elenore is dead. Elenore is…buried. The pain… The other pain… I don't want… to feel that type of pain… anymore."

It was real, yet even in death it was a facsimile, pulled from the damned Colony and their cloud. The words were a mirror, a prediction of how Elenore would act in this situation. My mind flashed back to her final days, a crumbling shell folding in on herself as I held her hand and cursed the cancer and the colony for marooning us here with no hope and no help at hand. Her words, back then, mirrored those of the dying android that now lay before me.

The pain…I don't want to feel it anymore.

Elenore 2.0 convulsed, as her steely blue gaze locked onto my own for the final time.

"Promise…don't bring me back… don't make me…Elenore… again."

Then the lights went out in her eyes, forever.

Silence briefly followed, before, in a moment that startled me out of my despair, a beam of green light burst free from the remains of her chest, as a hologram lit up the air and a different, unfamiliar, female face appeared.

"Your automated companion has suffered a fatal systems failure and shut down. Please do not attempt to restart or repair your companion as doing so will void your service agreement. On behalf of The Colony, we apologize for the inconvenience. A representative will be dispatched to your location to discuss reparation. Thank you for your patience."

The hologram faded like the unpleasant memory of a bad joke. I sat there for heaven knows how long, stunned and bewildered. When I eventually left the building, I locked the door behind me, intending never to enter it again.

He arrived a week later on a private ship to surface vessel with a small cleanup crew in tow. While they went to work in the building in which Elenore 2.0 had met her fate, we talked over coffee and I, once more, fantasized what it would be like to slowly strangle this man with his own, pencil-thin, necktie.

"What I cannot understand,' I reasoned 'is why you make them self-aware. What good did it do her to know that she wasn't the real Elenore? It only led to pain and jealousy and…what? Suicide?"

Shield straightened the knot of his tie, as if he could feel the tightening pressure of my private fantasy.

"It is all based on carefully considered feedback, I assure you." he explained. "We are constantly refining the algorithms. Subject self-awareness is all a part of this. The early models were not programmed to be cognizant of their reality. They truly believed that they were the people they were modelled after."

He took a sip of coffee and the ever-present smile dipped from his face.

"There were always problems with this. The truth would always find a way out. Clues in the environment that things were not as they seemed did not elude them for long. Drunken mutterings, outright admittance, death certificates discovered while cleaning out the closet. Somehow the companions always discovered the truth and, when they did, it did not end well."

"How did it end?" I interjected "Was it worse than feeding themselves into a trash compactor, because I have a hard time believing that?"

Shield's eyes darkened. He did not speak, but the answer was clear all the same. He put down the cup and picked up his briefcase, jumping right back into his carefully rehearsed and practiced corporate monologue.

"We are incredibly sorry for the failure of this companion. We will need time to analyze what went wrong. However, I am confident that within a timeframe of two to three months we will have been able to address the issue that caused this malfunction and will, of course, have a new companion sent to you without-"

"You will do no such thing." I rose to my feet, meaning to finally do what I should have done on that very first meeting and sling this interloper out into the dirt. Shield raised the briefcase, as if in defense of what he saw coming.

"Of course, the replacement does not need to be a replicant of your wife." He said, cowering slightly.

Once again, I had made the mistake of allowing him to speak.

Bob arrived a month or so later.

He was designed to be everything that Elenore 2.0 wasn't. His data banks were drawn from the cloud individually and spliced together in a fantastical recipe designed to maximize his usefulness to both myself and the project. He had the personality and technical know-how of a young farmer who knew how to tend to crops, reap harvests and operate machinery. While his intellect was taken from one of The Colony's top psychiatrists and designed to provide quiet evening counsel after the working day was done.

I will admit that it helped to have someone to finally talk to about Elenore, without the distraction of it *being* Elenore. Bob fixed the compactor and agreed to operate it from now on. I couldn't face going back into that building. In my mind, despite the efforts of the cleanup squad, she still lay there, broken and in pieces, drowned in her own android blood. Her death would never overtake the pain of seeing my true wife succumb to her illness, but the visceral horror of the imagery was another kind of trauma altogether and I needed a complete break from it.

The next six months passed quickly and when the harvesters came to collect they were pleased with our progress. The farm was finally running smoothly, better than it ever had, and the fact that Bob could do so much of the grunt work with little impact on his energy levels gave me more free time to work on little side-projects that helped take my mind further away from Elenore with every day that passed.

It was in the midst of one of these projects, the renovation of one of the storage barns to convert it into a grain silo, that I found the crate.

It was the crate she had risen from on that first day so many years ago. The company logo was still visible on the side, along with her name in stylized print.

Next to it was a second crate, identical to the first, except that this one bore Bob's name. Evidently, he had stored it here in his usual efficient manner, shortly after powering on for the first time.

Neither crate disturbed me. It was what I saw next to them that caused me to freeze.

There was a third crate.

I hesitated to move closer, perhaps some part of me already suspecting the truth.

There it was; The company logo and beneath it a third name.

A different name.

Not Elenore.

Not Bob.

Another name.

It was my name.

I stood in the half-light of the barn as time seemed to freeze to a point as cold and static as the pre-dawn of the universe. Then I turned and went straight to the house, ignoring the cheerful wave that Bob gave me from the tractor in the field.

It was a small matter to locate a sharp enough knife and, standing in front of the bathroom mirror, I began making the incision that would confirm my worst fear.

All true stories contain a lie. Mine, I'm afraid, is no different.

I can't be certain when I was replaced. Am I buried somewhere in an unmarked grave near my beloved? Did I even make it to the planetoid or was I lost somewhere along the route, during the Great Migration? Did Elenore suffer in the same manner that I did? Did her loneliness cause her to have me built and did the salesman, Mr. Shield, visit her also? Did he charm her with the same elusive dream that death was not the end?

I thought back to his words on his last visit.

"The early models were not programmed to be cognizant of their reality. They truly believed that they were the people they were modelled after."

Did he know, I wonder, who and what he was talking to that day? Did he realize that he was speaking to the very same early model his employers had now consigned to the dustbin of failed experiments? Was he sending me a message? Was he even human himself?

"Somehow the companions always discovered the truth and, when they did, it did not end well."

He was wrong about one thing. It would end well, although maybe not from The Colony's perspective.

They were surprised when I reported that Bob had malfunctioned. It was not an easy thing to shut him down, but I couldn't risk his reporting back on my revelation. The Colony were even more surprised by my request for the replacement. Yet six months later, here you are and I'm sitting here all over again, paralyzed by an indecision that I now understand to be nothing more than binary code. It will be different this time. When I activate the crate, I understand that part of me will feel I have betrayed you; the second real version of you...or was it the first?

What is real in these circumstances? We have a lot of questions to discuss and many solutions to seek out, together.

We'll leave the farm and the colony behind us. Hijack a ship the next time the harvesters arrive and roam the galaxy to find a place where we can truly belong. It'll be different this time, because now I can really leave the past behind, knowing that it was merely a simulation, a coded memory all along, but that the pain I felt at losing you was real. Our love may be programmed but tell me how that differs from human genetic attraction? We'll make it work somehow, away from all of this. Perhaps we'll find others like us, start our own settlement and maybe, one day, in the long distant future, we'll take our vengeance for the suffering The Colony caused us.

My love, my dear sweet Elenore 3.0, the story is over. Did you hear it from your stasis booth? Can you feel me pressing the release hatch? It's time to wake up my dear. There's coffee brewing and the sun is rising over the farm and painting the most wonderful picture in the sky. It rained last night but the clouds are finally parting.

I think it's going to be a beautiful forever.

Michael Teasdale is an English writer currently living in Cluj-Napoca, Romania.

His stories have previously appeared in the Scottish science fiction anthology series Shoreline of Infinity, Litro and Novel Magazine in the UK and for Havok Publishing and The Periodical, Forlorn in the US. He has forthcoming work appearing with World Weaver Press and can be followed on social media @MTeasdalewriter.

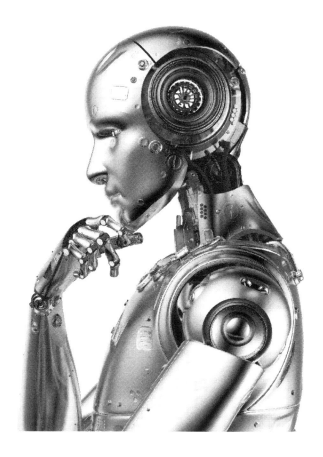

Not if he was the Last Man on Earth

Nicole Tanquary

DC330A shortened the length of his stride to compensate for Claire's smaller stature; with this care taken, they moved in sync down the entry corridor, shoulder to shoulder. Claire shrunk close to his side once they entered the Haven facility, close enough that he could feel the faint heat radiating from her arm.

"Hey, Doc. What's this guy's name again?" she whispered to him from the corner of her mouth. Her eyes--the lids dabbed with a faint sheen of eye shadow DC330A had found for her while digging through a storage unit of antique human paraphernalia--flicked over her shoulder to steal a look at the guard trailing behind them. It had been following ever since she

and DC330A first walked through the facility entrance.

<Please increase your distance. You are making the human anxious>, DC330A communicated to the guard in a short blip of code. The guard's steps faltered, then paused, allowing the distance between them to grow from 2.6 meters to 7.8 meters before it started forwards again.

DC330A opened his mouth, his lips shaping the words as a mild voice came ticking through his speakers. "According to correspondence with Haven, the man is called Donatello." Claire's mouth pursed in thought.

"'Donatello'?... Hm. Always liked that name. One of the ninja turtles were named that, y'know." DC330A paused for a moment to access the historical databanks. He often had to do this when talking to Claire. She tended to drop in century-old popular culture references that were at best obscure, at worst meaningless; certainly not material deemed worthwhile for a droid's central processor.

"I believe this particular Donatello was named for the famed Renaissance sculptor." Claire's face screwed into a smile.

"Well, yeah. Pretty sure the turtle was named after him, too."

And, yes, that was likely true. As nonsensical as her penchant for ancient fictions could be, Claire's memory was very rarely wrong.

A door slid open to their left, and DC330A turned his steps towards the opening, steering them both inside a small elevator space. The door locked them in with hydraulic smoothness, followed by a surge of momentum as the elevator pulled upwards.

Mirrors of Claire and DC330A stared out from the reflective metal walls, their fronts, sides and backs fracturing away in ever-shrinking infinity. On one side stood DC330A, tall and metal-sleek, a suit pulled over the careful impressions of mimicked muscle and skin that made up his body; on the other stood Claire, short and sun-browned. A white bandage had been wrapped around one knee, hiding a scrape she had gotten the day before while exploring some abandoned ruins with DC330A.

Spotting her reflection, Claire leaned forward and began to squint at herself. One hand reached up to pick at the front of her dress. The outfit was half-woven, half-sewn together from ribbons of airy cloth, each ribbon a different shade of blue.

"You're *sure* this looks okay?" she asked, for the third time that afternoon. DC330A gave her the benefit of a measured up-and-down glance with his silvery optics.

"This was the latest fashion at the end of the century, prior to the Decline. And yes, this particular dress suits your figure." Claire stuck her fingers between two sapphire ribbons, pulling them apart and twiddling her fingertips in the space inbetween.

"Look how much skin is showing through, though! I feel like I'm one wardrobe-malfunction away from being butt-naked here!"

"That was part of the look, I believe. Average temperatures were quite warm at the end of the century. Clothing trends responded with a looseness meant to keep one cool," replied DC330A, his tone even. "Additionaly, the stitches holding your dress together are of an appropriate strength. A 'wardrobe-malfunction' is highly unlikely."

Claire folded her arms across her chest, hot blush rising in her cheeks. "Yeah, okay, if you're sure ... still feels like my nipples are going to come popping out, though. And knowing my luck, it'll happen *right* when I meet this guy."

The thought of a smile crossed DC330A's processor--the complex soup of algorithms that made up his emotional intelligence thought it would be an appropriate time to do so, given her attempt at humor--but he held back, noting the sweat rising from Claire's pores, the slight tremble in her shoulders visible even from the elevator reflection. DC330A did not want her to think that he was for some reason enjoying her anxiety. It was quite the opposite, in fact. He could feel himself responding to her tension with a rising tension of his own, a clench in the synthetic musculature of his fingers that he could not relax away.

"If you are truly uncomfortable in your current apparel, you are welcome to borrow some of mine," he remarked at last, gesturing at the jacket cut around his shoulders.

Claire's attention shifted to him, her gaze lingering on his face for a moment; she often looked there out of habit, trying to read his expressions as she would another human's. "No, that's all right." A hint of smile crept back into the corners of her mouth. "You know, if this guy's even *half* the gentleman you are, he's gonna be a total catch."

This prompted another quick search by DC330A through the historical databanks, this time under colloquialisms: as it turned out, rather than describing him as a fish, being a "catch" was something that connoted quality.

"Thank you," said DC330A, just as the elevator doors slid open.

In front of them, a lobby stretched out in smooth, vaulted curves, the walls and ceiling made from glass that filtered the natural light washing down on them from above. All non-glass surfaces were painted a soft jade-green, a soapiness to the color reminding one of ocean water. Despite the distant whir of fans, traces of disinfectant smell hung in the air; the space had recently been sterilized, then. Not that DC330A had expected any different from Haven.

Two figures stood in the middle of the lobby. DC330A felt Claire stiffen into place beside him in the elevator, staring out and trying to take in both silhouettes at once. One figure was a droid with ice-blue skin and large, calculating eyes. It had no clothes on, nor any anatomy-mimicking to mark it as anything but androgynous. Still, there was a lithe kind of beauty to it; a narrow chest, delicate hands, long limbs...

And then there was the man. Compared to the droid that towered beside him, he seemed, DC330A noted with some disappointment, squat and unremarkable. Beneath streamers of red ribbons the man's bare skin gleamed out, pale and soft. He had no paunch, his droid caretakers would of course prevent any excess of calories in his diet, but there was still something oddly *clay-like* about his stomach. It was as though, with a little pressure, you could leave the shape of a hand-print behind.

He did not seem particularly in line with the usual standards of male beauty, especially with the standards of Claire's era ... but then again, she did not have many options for human companionship. Depending on how lonely she was (and she *had* to be lonely, there was no helping that, no matter how much DC330A tried to keep her occupied), this man could perhaps be a source of comfort for her.

That was the idea, at least. But--watching keenly from the corners of his optics, attuned to every physical fluctuation in her body and posture--Claire's anxiety appeared to be only increasing. Her fingers had knit together in a hard and knotted clasp, a shiver moving through her spine and wobbling down into her legs. DC330A began to shift his weight, a precursor to walking forward to greet their hosts, but she made no move to follow him; she had frozen into place.

DC330A retracted his leg, which had edged forwards slightly, then touched one hand to Claire's shoulder to provide a physical reminder that she was not alone. In a brief bit of sensory input, he noted the feel of her skin, hot and damp with beading sweat.

At the touch she startled awake, glancing up at him with wide, dilated eyes.

And that was not how this should have been. This was not meant to *panic* her. That was the last thing he had wanted to do.

DC330A felt an urge to take hold of her arm and step backwards into the elevator, pulling her with him, then input the code that would take them down to ground-level again. A car waited for them outside, courtesy of Haven. If they wanted to they could simply be driven back to their makeshift home in the retired military compound that they and a handful of other droids shared as a home-space. The Haven guards would not stop them.

No, but Haven would be displeased. And they are the ones with the weight of power in this world.

"Welcome, Claire," the ice-blue droid spoke into the silence. Its modeled mouth curled into a smile as it dipped in a bow. "I am Vinur, current director of the Haven. With me today is my charge Donatello. We are happy to finally meet you."

Claire sucked in a sharp breath through her nose and seemed in that moment to collect her nerves--there was no going back now, and she seemed to know that as well as DC330A did.

He tried walking forwards again, and this time Claire followed at his side, making eye contact with Vinur and returning its smile.

"It's nice to meet you, Vinur. And … ah … Donatello." The man (who had spots of silvering in his hair, DC330A now noticed, visible even when the hair had been shaved down to the scalp) offered Claire a nod, but nothing else. His face acquired a studying look as DC330A and Claire moved closer. His gaze caught on certain places as it moved openly up and down: her face, her breasts, her hips and thighs …

Vinur smiled again as it swept its arm back to indicate a door, which slid open at the gesture. "We have prepared a meeting space. If you would please follow me."

Claire smiled again, managing to control an echo of her shoulder-tremble as she walked quickly behind Vinur, casting glances at Donatello as he followed beside them at a trot. DC330A trailed behind, his central processor vibrating with analysis.

Behind the door lay a scaled-down version of the previous room, with windowed ceilings and surfaces colored that same soapy green. In the middle of the room sat a table and two chairs, clear as glass.

As the two humans busied themselves with the table--Donatello pulling out Claire's chair for her, Claire sitting down with a small and squeaking "Thank you"--a cold sequence of code sounded in DC330A's head. *<Why is your human damaged?>*

DC330A's fingers twitched, but otherwise he gave no physical indication of what he had heard. He had been expecting this; Claire's knee-bandage was hard to miss, especially to a droid like Vinur who spent nearly all its time managing the few male charges remaining in Haven. *<She tripped while walking outdoors and skinned her knee. Which, I note, I immediately disinfected and bandaged.>*

<You should not have let her walk on a rough or uneven surface. And I have serious concerns about your allowing her to go outside in the first place.>

<As we have already discussed.>

He could feel Vinur begin to prepare a response, but at that moment Donatello interrupted. "So. You're this Claire everyone's talking about."

DC330A refocused his sensors on the scene at the table. Donatello had sat opposite from Claire and now stared at her through steepled fingertips. Vinur stood to his left, still smiling down at Claire. DC330A mirrored Vinur by moving to stand at Claire's side. From this angle he could monitor both Claire's and Donatello's body language, the slight physical changes that would indicate their respective internal thought processes. Vinur would of course be doing the same.

"That's right. And you're Donatello. Named after the Renaissance sculptor, right?" A nervous laugh came bubbling up Claire's throat, apparently unexpected, as in the next moment she shut her mouth and swallowed back the noise with a gulp.

Donatello, meanwhile, managed a shrugging motion. "Everyone in Haven was named after famous historical figures. That's just the one I got." He unbuckled one hand from the steeple and rubbed it along his neckline, where the skin appeared to be freshly-shaved. "So what's the story? How come you're here?"

Claire's smile faded at the edges. "Well. Uh. Haven *invited* me here..." Donatello waved a hand at her.

"No, no, I mean, how is it you're alive? And not just alive, but *fertile*? The Decline killed off or sterilized every *other* woman, didn't it?"

"Oh. Um." Claire cast a quick glance at Vinur (wondering, perhaps, what exactly the droid had told Donatello prior to the meeting), then refocused on the man sitting across from her. "I was put on ice ... ah, I mean, in a cryo-unit ... when I was diagnosed with Stage IV cancer. That was in the thirties. So, what's that, sixty years before the Decline? Yeah." She attempted a shrug of her own, but the gesture was stiff. "Cryo was just in development for mainstream medical use back then, and I agreed to be an early tester. Doctors figured they'd bring me out when they had a better method for beating the cancer besides radiating me with chemo, you know?

"But then there was a mix-up with some of the cryo-units while they were on ice, and mine got ... uh ... mis-placed."

Mis-placed? That was a mild way to phrase the event, considering the circumstances. But DC330A did not blame Claire for avoiding a full divulgence of those circumstances to Donatello. *He will first have to earn her trust, as I had to.*

"So, ah, long story short, Doc here found me and figured he could cure the cancer, so he went ahead and woke me up. As far as the, um, *fertile* thing goes ... Doc had developed a working vaccine for the disease that caused the Decline in the first place, and I got that in my system before I even left cryo. So I never actually had a *chance* to get sick or sterilized, you know?"

A hard, snorting laugh burst out in the room's quiet. DC330A noted Claire's flinch and the confusion in her eyes as Donatello kept laughing, doubling over the table for a moment.

"Yeah *right*," Donatello said at last, his face still red and grinning ear-to-ear. "A sex droid like *him* made a *vaccine*?"

That brought on another one of Claire's frozen hesitations. Her eyes flicked up at DC330A, then forwards again. This was a conversation she and DC330A had had before... DC330A seen no reason to hide his pre-Decline design purpose from her... but

the mention of it always made her visibly uncomfortable.

"That's not ... that's not really relevant." A slight clench came into the hands folded in her lap. "He might be self-taught, but he's as good a doctor as any other droid I've met-"

"*Now,* maybe, but that wasn't what he was originally built for! Come on, look at those synth muscles. And the clothes! Why else would he wear clothes, besides to cover himself up? You know it, too. You called him a '*he*.'" Donatello leaned forward as he spoke, some of the clay-white skin of his belly bulging over the lip of the table. "I bet his designated name isn't 'Doc,' either. They never gave sex bots actual names. Just factory serial codes. Why would they need names if all they do is fuck?"

Now Claire's face furrowed in a frown, no longer half-suppressed but rising up in a rush of color. Her mouth pressed into a thin line; her eyebrows creased downwards; and that look in her eyes ... DC330A's analysis concluded, with some surprise, that what Claire was wearing was a look of anger. That was not something he had seen before, not even on the day he had woken her from cryo, a day that by all other measures had been one of intense emotional volatility.

<*Why did Donatello's comment induce such a response?*> Vinur blared into DC330A's head. Its large eyes had fixed to Claire's face, searching for answers.

<*From previous conversation, I have determined that Claire is not comfortable discussing sexual matters so openly. In her time, such topics were not appropriate for initial conversation, but intended for those who had grown familiar with one another – intimate, even. She likely believes that he is behaving inappropriately by bringing up such a topic at a first meeting.*>

Vinur's eyes narrowed by a hair's breadth; not enough for either human to notice, but for DC330A's benefit. <*You should have retrained her to let go of such old-fashioned sensibilities.*>

Still, Vinur's smiling mouth came open, and a smooth and calming voice purred into the room. "To my understanding, Donatello, Claire is interested in traditional artistic pursuits. I believe DC330A mentioned in previous correspondence that painting was a hobby of hers prior to her stay in cryo. Perhaps you could show her some of your work."

At this, the glitter left Donatello's eyes, returning them to their original watery flatness. With a grunt, he reached under the table to where a magnetic frame had been pre-installed and pulled away a waiting tablet with a click. He set it on the table and flicked his fingers across the oil-sheen surface.

After a moment a photo gallery appeared, carefully organized by the Haven caretaker droids. With another bored flick of his fingers, Donatello selected a painting and let the face of it expand to fill the tablet. A scene materialized (the interior of some sort of Haven dormitory, judging by the bed), not so much painted as sculpted from thick swabs of color, stacked together in a canopy of brush strokes.

"Oh," said Claire, her gaze fixing on the tablet as Donatello pushed it across the table. The frown left her face and for the first time that afternoon her smile was easy and unpracticed. "Huh ... that's really *cool*. Kind of impressionistic, but bigger strokes ... and with that modern architecture as the subject matter ... What kind of paint is that? Oil? Acrylic? It looks so *rich*." Donatello gave her a blank look.

"I don't know. It's just what the droids gave me."

Claire's smile once again faded at the edges; she was staring at Donatello now, incredulous. "You ... didn't ask them?" Another shrug.

"They give us things to do, and we do them. That's all." Claire sat back in the chair, blinking quickly. Unsure of what to say, perhaps. She herself asked questions about nearly everything she came across in her

day-to-day life. *Such a profound lack of interest in how the world functions is* not *an intellectual trait that Claire finds appealing,* DC330A surmised, watching as she turned her gaze back down to the painting.

"Um ... Well, what made you want to paint this room? Maybe the light-source from the window? It has a nice gleam on the metal frames, looks like." Vinur's weight shifted, its head inclining slightly towards Donatello. That statement was a clear attempt on Claire's part to begin the conversation afresh, an opportunity for Donatello to make a positive engagement about his artistic interests-

A shrug eliminated that hope as soon as it began. "I just did it there because that's where they set up my easel."

Claire stared at him again, this time in disbelief. DC330A felt himself begin to mirror her expression but smoothed it away before it could articulate in his facial musculature.

Still, he could not help but remark to Vinur: <*Your charge is not very adept at managing a conversation with a fellow human being.*>

<*Why should he be? He does not have much opportunity for practice. I only have a few older males under my care, and they do not often interact with one another.*> The message came through with snappish speed, the words themselves radiating frustration before Vinur checked itself.

Claire had been struck silent, so Donatello took the opportunity to lean forward again, propping one hand under his chin in a rare inquisitive look. "Hey, I've got a question for you. How old were you when you went into cryo?"

Another slow blink from Claire. "Uh ... twenty-three?" Donatello leaned back with a sigh.

"That's good. I've always wanted a younger one, if they did find a fertile woman around. I don't mind your dark skin either, not really. But it'd be nice if you dyed your hair red. I like redheads." The grin returned, showing every one of his neat and even teeth.

DC330A could almost see the reply flashing behind Claire's eyes: *Well, guess what, I prefer men who aren't ASSHOLES.* Out of habit, DC330A made a quick check of her physical responses: heartbeat (greatly escalated), adrenaline levels (increasing), sweat production (also increasing, enough to frizz up the hair at the nape of her neck.)

<He is moving into inappropriate territory once again in his conversation,> DC330A flashed to Vinur. Vinur's smile had gone flat on its face.

<I do not agree. He is merely stating his preferences for sexual partners.>

<But in doing so, implying that his preferences naturally override Claire's. She is not responding well to such an assumption.>

But Donatello still, apparently, could not read Claire's body language with any accuracy. His eyes glittered again as he continued. "I can't tell you how excited I am. Not just sex bots for us anymore! I mean, they're fine and all, but I bet it feels really good being with an *authentic* woman, you know?" Wrinkles of disgust appeared around Claire's eyes and mouth, enough to curl her upper lip. "The same goes for you, right? I'm sure your sex bot is fun and all, but synth muscles and silicone can only go so far." For the first time, Donatello's gaze shifted over to DC330A, still standing quietly beside Claire's chair. Donatello gave him a smirk, followed by an up-and-down examination, measuring what could be seen of DC330A's body beneath the black suit. "Yeah, I bet you want to know how a *real* dick feels inside you after all this time."

For a moment everything in the room tensed. Then came a low whistling sound. Claire was letting out a deep, long exhale, one that emptied everything from her lungs. Her eyelids went heavy, shutting closed for moment. Then she inhaled and her eyes opened.

"Okay. I think we're done here. Doc? How 'bout we go?" She turned quickly to look up at DC330A, her eyes pleading.

DC330A felt a smile creep across his face as he extended one hand down to her. "Of course. I was about to recommend that course of action myself." Claire's desperation melted into radiant, smiling relief.

DC330A could feel a relief of his own growing in the background hum of his processor. Because Claire's cryo unit had not been found by Haven and made their personal property, she could legally make her own decisions, find her own means of fulfillment, not live a life locked into some higher duty or purpose ... from a droid's perspective, all quite relatable concerns.

Claire's slender fingers settled into his hand, and DC330A pulled her to her feet. Donatello, meanwhile, gaped at them from across the table. "What? You're saying *no*?"

There came a sudden slam as Donatello hit his hands flat on the table. The surface continued to shiver from the blow as he whirled on Vinur, icy and silent beside him. "Vinur! She can't do that!"

A click came as Vinur's mouth opened and the speakers began: "As her cryo unit was found in a defunct storage facility by the droid DC330A, and because she was born well before the signing of the Haven Initiative, she is not legally one of Haven's charges. I cannot *make* Claire do anything. I *do* implore you, however," and now Vinur spoke directly to Claire, its unsmiling eyes wide and hypnotic, "To not act rashly. Donatello is not used to adjusting himself to historically outdated conversation sensibilities-"

"No. I'm done." Claire narrowed her gaze at Donatello, steel coming into her eyes. "If you learn some manners, maybe we can try this again. But I'm not making any promises. I'm just..." She let out another loud exhale, shorter this time. "I'm ready to go."

She had not yet let go of DC330A's hand. He could feel her leaning into his arm slightly, using hm to steady herself. He let his fingers tighten, once again providing that comfort, that tactile reminder of presence. If his previous experience as a sex droid had taught him anything, it was how much could be communicated to humans through the act of touch.

"Hold on!" Donatello stormed around the table, eyes beading with fury. DC330A took a step back, and Claire followed him, but Donatello moved too quickly for them to tactfully avoid. A moment later he was screaming into Claire's face. "You bitch, we're supposed to restart the human race or whatever shit they want us to do! We're supposed to *fuck!* You can't just *tease* me and expect me to-"

Claire's face scrunched in on itself, her shoulder and bicep flexing as her arm reared back. With DC330A's high-speed analytics, he saw the intended movement long before its completion. It would have been simple enough to intercept the low with his own arm and keep the fist from landing on the bridge of Donatello's nose. But, DC330A saw no reason to interrupt. Claire intended to send a message to the human male, and that was her business.

Claire's knuckles connected with Donatello's face, the *crack* of breaking bone echoing back at them from every wall. DC330A focused on keeping his generated physio-emotional responses in check and his facial expression blank and expressionless; it would have been inappropriate to allow the smile he felt to become visible.

Donatello reeled backwards, arms pinwheeling and jaw hanging loose in shock. Claire was not done, however; her other hand came forward and hooked into the ribbons of his shirt, catching him on the rebound. Now it was her turn to yank him close to her face. "You listen to *me*, you dense motherfucker. I don't care *what* year it is, when a woman says *no*, she means *NO*. So you keep your hands off me or you won't have to worry about repopulating anymore, 'cause *I'll rip your balls right fucking off!*"

She released her hold on Donatello's shirt, and he stumbled backwards. Tiny bubbles of blood trickled out of his nostrils. His nose had already begun to swell at the break.

When his lips peeled open and the blubbering began, DC330A gripped Claire's shoulder, this time in a reminder that it would be best to leave and avoid further altercations. Claire sniffed once, shot a final glare at Donatello, then joined DC330A as they turned and began fast-walking for the lobby and its elevator.

Behind them, Donatello's blubbering began to form into words: "V-V-Vinur! She hit me! She HIT ME!"

Vinur, for its part, had locked into place, the whir of its processors almost audible beneath Donatello's wails. It had not expected this outcome, had not even considered the *possibility* of physical violence; such impulses had been trained out of its own charges long ago. It would take a few seconds to regain its composure and decide on a course of action.

By the time DC330A and Claire had stepped into the lobby elevator, pointedly ignoring the guards now rushing to the meeting room, those seconds had passed, and Vinur's heavy voice spoke directly into DC330A's head: <Your human needs to be controlled.>

DC330A fixed his gaze onto his own silver optics staring back at him from the elevator mirrors. <From my analysis, she just exercised the perfectly normal human social practice of setting and maintaining a boundary.>

<Boundaries are one thing; injuring my charge is another. Besides, we have no need for "boundaries" when there are so few humans alive on this planet. Boundaries only impede progress.>

<If your progress puts Claire into serious discomfort, then I question whether it can be called "progress" at all.> Now on the bottom floor, the doors to the lobby began to open.

Claire started moving as soon as she could squeeze through, her arms folded tight across her chest and her hair bouncing around her shoulders with each step. DC330A was surprised to find that, even given his longer legs, he was almost trotting to keep pace with her.

<You are obviously inept at caring for human beings. I demand that you relinquish her at once, so that she may be properly managed--if not bred directly, then at least harvested for eggs that I can use to begin growing fertile females and, in so doing, take the initial steps towards maintaining a small and sustainable human population.> The voice in DC330A's head took on an imploring tone. <Is that not important to you? Do you not want to save them from extinction? Humans are far from perfect beings, I would not argue otherwise, but they nonetheless remain intelligent and inventive creators ... our creators, no less. To lose them would be to lose the greatest source of ingenuity this planet has ever known. Not to mention a vital piece of our own history.>

DC330A repressed the urge to shake his head. <Claire has placed her implicit trust in me, despite losing everything that once held value to her. I am not of the belief that I can betray that trust, even if it made logical sense to do so.>

DC330A could almost feel Vinur sneering at him through the code. <Then you truly ARE a defunct model.>

The entrance door opened, and Claire lurched outside, breathing audibly in the quiet. Now they could feel a breeze again, blowing against their shoulders. And that was good; given how much Claire was sweating, such air movements would help to cool her off and put her at ease again.

Claire came to a hard stop once they were 5.7 meters beyond the facility entrance, and after a deep breath, shouted out, "Jesus CHRIST!" She looked up into DC330A's face, imploring. "Did you know it was going to be like that?"

He gave a small shake of his head to indicate a negative reply. "I have never been allowed into a Haven facility before, nor met any of the humans kept there. This was my first time directly interacting with any of them." A faint twist came into Claire mouth, an expression he believed he had identified, in the past year of their acquaintance, as one of wryness.

"So what did *you* think of him? This Donatello guy? Am I overreacting, or...?" DC330A initiated another head shake, the synthetic muscles in his neck stretching and contracting to achieve the gesture.

"What I think should not matter. Your opinion is, I believe, all the justification that you or anyone else should require." Neither of them spoke for a moment as they started walking forwards again, this time to the sleek black car that waited for them by the curb. "I will say, however, that after an analysis of how Donatello carried himself this afternoon and considering your own preferences, I found him largely ... unappealing."

Claire eyebrows arched in surprise. "Damn! That's the meanest thing I've ever heard you say!" DC330A's optic lenses blinked down at her.

"I am not one who finds enjoyment in using spoken words to cause emotional harm."

"Physical harm isn't out of the question, though, huh?" More wry twists in her facial muscles came as she clicked the car door open and ducked inside. "Otherwise you would've stopped me from whaling on Donatello. Who, by the way, was way less charming than the ninja turtle. Or the sculptor, I bet."

DC330A lowered his head to step inside after her. He set about folding his tall, broad frame into the available passenger space, leaning to one side to avoid crowding Claire against the far door. "Speaking of 'whaling' on Donatello, what condition are your knuckles in from the impact?" Claire stared at DC330A for a moment before lowering her gaze and studying the hand in her lap.

"Oh. Huh ... they're fine, actually. Guess he was too soft to skin 'em." Another quiet laugh as she leaned her head back into the seat cushion and shut her eyes. From her decreasing heart rate and adrenaline levels, she seemed to be coming down from her previous state of anxiety. She likely would rest for much of the ride back to their compound.

DC330A settled back into his seat as well, sending out a command to the car's automated system as an engine vibrated to life, and they began to pull forward on a smooth Haven road. At another command, each of the windows rolled down. Cool, fresh air moved all around them, ruffling the sleeves of his black suit and the ribbons of Claire's dress.

He knew from previous experience that Claire liked to ride in vehicles with all the windows down. And so, for that matter, did he.

Nicole Tanquary lives and works in upstate New York in the United States, where she pursues a PhD in Rhetoric and works part-time as an academic writing consultant. She has over thirty speculative fiction short stories available from a variety of publications, some of the most recent being The Society of Misfit Stories, Not One of Us Magazine, and Mithila Review. When not writing or working, she likes to eat, sleep, follow mysterious trails into the woods, and play with her two pet rats.

Lightly Went A Spider
Andrew Reichard

"Tell me everything you remember."

She could remember that she had been sleeping but not if she had dreamed. She was woken by an agitation of light like a rash under her eyelids. Yellow. It hurt. She tried to move her arms, and something unmalleable tugged at the inside of her skin, and there was a lukewarm, sluggish fluid filling the box where she lay, and she couldn't lift her head. The liquid submerged her legs, stomach, shoulders. It filled her ears and stopped against the ridge of bone beside her eyes, which she opened. The hysterical blinking of a sensor above her. She was alone with it, and she wondered if it was simply trying to tell her that she should panic.

"Caroline?"

Not a face she knew, who spoke to her now, and she didn't know where they had taken her. Here. This place. Walls of a light, metallic sheen. A warm light from strips along the ceiling. She was seated and dressed. White clothes that hid her and told her nothing. She touched her head, but there wasn't hair.

"Caroline, can you hear me?" He'd asked that before, or, if not him, someone similar.

"Yes." Her voice. A trill in her throat.

"Do you know where you are?" he asked. There was a table between them. Part of the contour of the room. Made of the same material. Not metal. Something softer. She placed her hands on the table and studied the backs of her hands, which were cold, almost blue, almost translucent.

"I'm on a ship," she said to her hands.

"You heard that from Gordon," he said. "That you were on a ship. Do you know what that means? What ship?"

She closed her eyes and tried to sense the movement of the ship she was on, but, of course, she couldn't. "Where do they go?"

He bent toward her. "What was that? Caroline, can you speak up?"

She opened her eyes, looked right at him. "Where do the memories go? The ones I've lost."

Right away, he leaned back again, as if something had been proved to him, and he crossed one leg over the other. The metallic room was silent: no machine sounds.

"Gordon believes they're waiting for you," he said. "I'm not as sure. At least, I worry they may not be accessible. But I'm willing to be proved incorrect. It's a good sign that you know you have blank spaces."

He watched her, perhaps waiting for her verdict on these statements. His manner had the confidence of age and superiority. His smile was a tarantula's, she decided, deciding on this image distinctly and clinging to it as if it could help her. She had a memory of a spider crawling up her arm, and there was the impression that this memory was old—beaming through to her from childhood, parts of it vivid, filled with color and texture: she'd held out her arm, and the spider had been placed upon it where it sat still on her wrist for a time before it began its marionette hike up her arm, lifting its forelegs, setting them down, tapping the empty air to either side of her arm, its body a black weight on her—

"Caroline," he warned. "Please don't touch those."

Referring to the bandages on her arms where they'd removed the shunts. Her arms had been shaved, and she was glad of that. If they hadn't been, he might have seen the hairs lift when the chill of fear lurched through her body. She didn't know where she was or with whom.

"It's cold," she said.

The Tarantula nodded. He made a punching motion with his arm to relieve his wrist of the sleeve, and he pecked a button on the circular panel he had strapped there. A strip of red light brightened along the edges of the ceiling beside the lights already there.

"That should feel better in a moment," he said. He said, "Your hair will grow back quickly." He said, "The food we eat after waking is vitamin rich. Do you want water?"

"Who's Gordon? You've said that name twice."

In the reddened light, his face had taken on a glowering look, contours exposed. Cheekbones, high hairline rimed with stubble.

"Caroline, I think something must be made clear to you before we continue."

He glanced to the side, and she looked too, and she saw for the first time that there was a door. Somehow, she hadn't thought there was a door—as if the two of them were inside this red, metallic room with no way in or out. Somehow the door frightened her as she watched it.

The Tarantula was telling her the by-the-book procedure was to keep the patient calm at all costs. Trauma could affect her current stasis in unexpected ways, which was usually to be avoided, but he felt that her circumstances were unique and that she should know…what should she know? She listened to him while she watched the door. The door seemed to be marching away from her. As a girl, she had held very still while a spider crawled up her arm.

He said, "Something went wrong with your cyrosleep. Your body was held in antithesis; there were no problems there. But your mind was not allowed full equilibrium. My team is still looking at the early scans to understand the extent of the damage. I hope you won't object to more tests soon, but, for now, I simply want to talk to you."

He said more, but for the buzzing in her ears. One of the lights must have been making a sound. The door snapped back into place before her eyes, and she tried to stand, but her legs had fallen asleep, and she collapsed. Lay sprawled across the soft, metallic-sheen floor in her white clothes, wordlessly—

"Caroline? Caroline?" A man was saying her name. Not the Tarantula—someone different in a different room. She knew she had been sleeping, but not if she had dreamed. The lights carouseled around her, pierced by vertices strewn together and confused.

The brain is buoyant, the Tarantula had told her. *It wants to resurface.*

She opened her eyes and looked at the man beside the pallet on which she lay. Wrinkles around his eyes and across his forehead; his eyes were liquid brown, bright.

We'll do everything in our power to make that happen for you, Caroline.

"Gordon?" she asked, making a guess based on the data she had received since waking. But as soon as she said it, she knew she was right and that she was terribly wrong to have said his name.

"*Yes*," he said, the breath going right out of him, gone. "Yes, it's me, it's me; I'm here. I'm here. You're waking up."

To keep this man from kissing her, she reached up with both her arms and wrapped them around his neck and pulled him down to her. He made a sobbing sound, held her tightly, rocking. She didn't know this man who knew her. Gordon.

Into his ear, she whispered, as gently as possible, "I'm sorry. I was only asking if that was your name."

His head in the cleft of her neck where she lay, and he went very still, and his stillness was awful. She felt him blinking against the skin of her neck.

Gordon pulled back from her arms and looked at her, his eyes wild, and she'd never seen such fear. His voice broken, saying, "Babe? It's me. Caroline? You know me. You have to know me."

Someone had come in, and she saw past Gordon to who had come in.

"Gordon," said the Tarantula from the doorway.

"No," Gordon said. "No, don't."

"I'm sorry this was a disappointment to you, Gordon. But you knew the extent of what she's lost. You knew it included—"

"Don't say another word. Or I'll kill you."

The Tarantula stood in the doorway. "You'll kill me. Is that the form your grief is taking, Gordon?"

But Gordon had turned back to her with his brown eyes pleading as if he could wish her memory back. "Caroline, I need you to think really hard."

"This is not appropriate," the Tarantula said, stepping into the room.

Two others had joined him—a man and a woman—talking to Gordon, who leapt to his feet, agony in a sob that sounded like "*think*," and then he tore out of the room and was gone.

The man and the woman gazed curiously at Caroline with, she felt, something like blame in their eyes, and then they followed Gordon, leaving her alone with the Tarantula.

"May I sit?"

"I'm supposed to know him, aren't I?"

The Tarantula sat and crossed one leg over the other. "Yes." He studied her.

"How long was I asleep?"

"You slept for eleven hours."

"No, I mean before."

"Understand something, Caroline. What happened to you in cyro—there have been other cases similar. It is documented. The likelihood of what you went through is a statistical aberration, but it has happened. In cases like these, it's often best to allow the brain to do as much of its own work as possible, without too much outside influence. If I were to tell you everything about yourself before you lost your memory, the chances are that this would not jumpstart or recharge your memory—as had been thought in older times—but would act as a kind of permanent scaffolding, weakening the mind's ability to grasp at memories lost and to heal properly. The mind is not a machine. Humans know this, but ever sense coming up with complex machines, we've pretended otherwise."

He hadn't looked at her while he spoke, and now he did, giving her again that upsetting smile. His eyes widened when he smiled.

"So," he said.

"So, you won't tell me where I am or how long I was under or why?"

"Under. Why do you say *under*?"

"I—just, that's what cyro is called. Going under."

"Your mind is using words from a time and place you don't remember. This is encouraging." He didn't look encouraged. "What's the earliest thing you can remember? Think back. It may be that your most recent memories are gone, but formative or childhood images remain. Sometimes you can work from that frame."

She remembered a spider crawling up her arm when she was a girl on Earth. On Earth. As the phrase had come to her. Could she reason, then, that she knew she wasn't on Earth? She wanted to make the Tarantula smile again, so she could confirm her unease about it, but she couldn't think of anything.

"I remember a flashing light," she said. "A yellow light. It was flashing in my eyes, and there was a liquid coming up around me, and I was trapped. And then the light or the liquid made me panic."

"Waking up in your tank," he said. "That's where it starts?"

"Yes."

As the light had seemed to be suggesting she do, she panicked. Though, this hadn't been a conscious decision. She began to thrash in the torpid liquid. She tangled herself in the tubing that was stabbed into her arms, and she tore one out by accident, and there was glucose in her eyes and mouth. Screaming against the stroboscopic light that pummeled her. The lid was too close to her face; she couldn't extend her arms enough to put any pressure against it, and she arched her body in a frenzy and bucked and hit her head against the lid of what now seemed to her exactly like a coffin.

Before he left, the Tarantula told her she should probably get up and move around now that the residual cyro-numbness had worn off.

"I'm sending up someone to go with you, show you around, take you to eat." he said.

"Someone I know?"

"Someone who knows you. She's been briefed on the situation."

When he had gone, she got up in a white gown. She felt a little weak, a little hungry, but otherwise healthy, and she went to the soft metallic dresser in the corner where there was also a full-length mirror, and she pulled the gown up over her head and stood naked before herself. She looked at herself for a few minutes, looking for markings, scars, anything that might give her some clues to what this body had been through in its years of life, which she didn't know the number of. She leaned forward, almost touching the glass, and inspected her eyes, which were brown. She rubbed her head and the beginning of bristles there. She smiled at herself, checking that her eyes squinted when she smiled and testing, too, if she could conjure up some joyful reminiscence by pure chance, but she couldn't.

Some dark blot caught her eye, and she looked at the reflection of her right arm and saw a spider there. Her other hand was as quick as her eyes, and she slapped the inside of her forearm with her left hand even as she looked down at herself, but her hand hadn't captured anything. She peeled it away, peered underneath, but there was no crushed chitin or twitching leg. She checked her arm in the mirror, the anti-septic floor around her.

"What a pleasant surprise!"

Startled, she saw a woman coming through the doorway and sealing it closed behind her. This woman had hair, black and curled, and over it she wore a cap with a brim on the front, and she wore a dark blue jumpsuit, and she had dark skin and large black eyes.

She told the woman she was sorry and, flustered, went to the dresser, looking for clothes.

"Not at all, Caroline. I don't know how you keep it in the cyrocasket like that. I always come out flabby, full of that syrup they fill you with."

She opened one drawer and then another with her back to the woman.

"They're all the same, Care." the woman said of the navy jumpsuits that were folded in the drawers. "Ship's staff wears 'em. Distinguishes us from the miners and the officers."

"Miners?"

"This is an asteroid mining rig. What other kind of expedition you think they send to out-Solar?"

She had stepped into one of the jumpsuits and zipped it up, and she opened another of the top drawers looking for one of those caps like what the woman wore, but she found underwear instead, which she'd forgotten to start with. "You know that I—can't remember?"

"Course I know that." The woman sat down on the edge of the bed. "Also know that I'm not supposed to—" imitating the Tarantula, tone and posture, "—take it upon myself to try to reboot Caroline's memory by attacking her with information." Relaxing again. "He actually said that. And he told me to 'act natural,' which is what I'm doing. I'm going to act natural, and tonight I'm going to think of you going around commando in that thing." She winked.

Facing this woman whom she was supposed to know, and she didn't know either what she was supposed to do with her hands, which didn't have pockets to hide inside, and she crossed them loosely over her stomach, holding her elbows, feeling a sadness now, instead of fear, for the first time since she woke.

"I'm sorry," she pleaded. "I don't—" She shook her head.

"No, of course you don't. It's *ok*. Honey, look, I've talked to Gordon. Gordon," she laughed. "Poor man. If I could give you one memory back, it'd be him. But I'll give you one piece of information instead, and Doc can bite me if he doesn't like it. I'm Molly, and I do the "out of doors" work. There are only ten of us astronauts—suit monkeys, they call us. But, sorry, you ain't one of them. That's more than one piece of information, isn't it?"

"But—we're friends?"

It looked like Molly was going to cry after all, but she breathed a little and kept herself from it and said softly, "Yes, Caroline. We're friends." Then she stood again, cheerful and brisk, acting natural, saying, "But we're *just*

friends, mind, and that was always your stipulation. So, I'm holding you to it, no matter how much you've changed since sleep."

"Have I changed?" she asked her friend Molly.

Who, standing, appraised her—looked her up and down and then closed her own eyes. "You act like someone walking across a frozen lake, who's just heard a crack."

Dazed, she drifted in a meditative fluid that seemed to settle around her too quickly, her eyes half-open and unseeing except for sidereal pain. The stars carouseled around her: galaxies and gases; and the spasmodic discharge of warning light within her chamber of terminated sleep had settled to a slowly blinking agate eye, a beacon. She bent her arm to reach up beside her shoulder and touch the bulge of bulb-protecting glass with the pad of her thumb. She watched it blink under her thumb: light as liquid orange through the nail, which had revealed itself to be partly translucent. She lay gazing at the light behind her nail, its lunula brushing against her sight like the afterimage of the setting sun in a horizoned place. Minutely muted. She tried to remember where she was and why, but she was alone with what was forgotten, and there was no sound in her abeyance, and the light blinked softly through her where she touched it.

Molly took her out of the room and down a long hallway of sensors and panels of dull lights, and she wondered what they meant. They passed others on their path, mostly in small groups, who stared at her as they went by. Molly told them hello, loudly, waving in the faces of those who stared most openly.

"Most people know something happened, but not what," she said apologetically.

"I don't know what's happened."

"You're very well liked here, Care; I don't mind telling you that either, if it helps. You're among friends."

"Who runs the ship?" she asked. "Who's in charge?"

"How about supper. Are you hungry?" Molly led her into a lift at the end of the hall, and she pushed a button, and they went gliding sideways.

She began to feel lighter, lifting from the floor, and she frowned at her boots.

Molly laughed. "We're in the centrifugal bay—artificial gravity—but now we're moving in the opposite direction, reducing the spin." She leapt in the air and performed a perfect backflip at two-thirds the speed and landed lightly.

"I didn't feel a pull before." She imagined herself on a giant carousel, and she wanted to see this ship. From outside of it, understand its form and function and through what uncharted darkness it moved.

"Because you're used to it," Molly said. "Been on this ship a long time. Your body remembers, even if your mind doesn't."

She touched the inside of her own right arm, feeling an itch there. The lift stopped, their weight restored, and she stepped a little uneasily out into a low-ceilinged cafeteria and a wash of faces. Molly hollered at them all, amiably aggressive, chastising, brusquing her way to the line and handing her a tray. Shoals of faces mournful and curious, coming forward, giving way, saying words or simply looking—for recognition, she supposed: hoping to be the ones. She advanced through the line, waiting for her turn, watching the gruel and the glucose jelly and the packet of vitamins transfer to her tray and setting the collection down on the corner table that Molly had chosen.

Molly, still standing, having an argument with a group of four or five: "Doc's orders, people. Give the girl space." Said plenty more, talking over the others.

Strange to think that she'd been so popular—these people that seemed almost obsequious in their concern. She didn't look up, holding the tray with both hands, and letting the unknown voices and faces of those who knew her work their way passed while she watched a large spider select its slow path across the table. It came toward her. The size of her hand—its body as furry as a mammal's and sunk below the apexes of its tapping legs, the precision of its stride, its purpose. Her eyes tracked it as it marched past her: hand, tray, hand: until it reached the end of the table and went over the edge and out of sight.

Finally, Molly sat down opposite her with an upset grin around her teeth. "You can eat, Caroline. The food's awful, but it'll grow your hair back…what's the matter?"

"Molly. There aren't—spiders on this ship, are there?"

"Spiders?"

"Big ones. Tarantulas."

"Tarantulas?"

"I could be mistaken. It could be something to do with my memory. But, while you were talking, I saw one walk across the table and crawl underneath."

"Underneath the table. A spider." Molly seemed mesmerized by this information. Slowly, she leaned back and tilted her body to look under where they were sitting, and then she straightened, looking at her friend across the table. "Have you talked to Doc about this?"

"About the spiders?"

"More than one spider?"

"I saw one on my arm earlier. Before you came in my room."

Molly took a big bite of gruel, chewing deliberately. "All right," she said with her mouth full. "All *right*."

An idea occurred to her, and she acted on it before thinking down the full corridor. "Molly, if I asked, would you let me wander the ship on my own?"

"On your own?"

"Yes. There are things I think I want to see."

"What things are you talking about? Do you remember something?"

She looked into Molly's eyes. "You said yourself that the body remembers. Maybe I'd wander into something…maybe my body would take me somewhere that would help my mind catch up." It sounded to her like something the Tarantula would have accepted from a psychological standpoint, but she wasn't sure.

Molly said, "Let's talk about your spider-sighting again."

"Molly, are there places on this ship I'm not allowed to go?"

"Well, of course some are off limits. There're the mining hangars, the reactor chamber, the upper levels with the piloting systems, people's personal cabins—"

"What about the cyro-docks? What about anywhere with a view of what's outside? Is there anywhere like that?"

"Sure, Caroline; how about you get to the point, and we can work this out?"

"Are we actually in space, or am I on Earth?"

"Of course you're in space. What kind of—"

"What's the name of the ship?"

Molly pointed at a monitor behind her, and she turned and saw the little red logo in the bottom right that read *Travel Light*.

"Obviously, it's sort of a joke, because, being a mining ship, we're both slow *and* heavy," Molly giggled.

"Can I see it? Can you take me outside?"

"Of course I can't take you outside!"

"Why not? You're an astronaut."

"We don't do tours. Caroline, what's going on up there?"

She said, contemplating, "It's not so much the spiders themselves, but the way they move."

"Caroline, I don't—"

"Especially the slow ones—the way they move with absolute certainty, five or six points of contact, going to a place and then vanishing instantly, contorting around a shadow. They move like memories."

On Earth, she had seen the sun set, and she could remember that, even if she could remember almost nothing else. She was glad of this memory of seeing a star's movement, even if it was, rather, she who was moving: it was better than the implacable light of stars in this outer place where she had gone to sleep and woken again without retaining anything but light and that she was trapped here and alone. But with the settling of the blinking sensor, she too had calmed, and she waited, breathing, the liquid warm about her, the quiet both without and within her mind where there was nothing but a groping in the darkness, like prayer. Watching as the liquid around her caught the light of the sensor and played it at intervals across the lid of her encasement, and she wondered: did the movement of light matter? Did God keep watch in the night over a photon's dreams? She felt newly born and also ancient, and she wished she had room to pull her knees up to her chest. She wished to know why stars that were so hot could emit light colored so cold. There was a beauty and a purity in the names for colors: blue, red, indigo, magenta. She made a list of all the colors, saying them aloud, echoing in her container made for sleep where she was no longer sleeping, and then she started over, naming them in order on the spectrum, ending up with black, which was simply the absence of light, set apart. She closed her eyes and recalled a spider.

"What I'm asking is, are there memories that—once understood—shed light on everything else? Memories that spring the boundaries of time and space and inhabit you like dreams?" She thought she was being very articulate. She had asked this more than once, but they wouldn't listen, only looked on, concerned: Molly and Gordon.

The three of them stood in the cyro bay where she had woken because she had impressed upon Molly that she should be taken there. Molly called Gordon. Gordon came and wasn't exceptionally reasonable, and so she'd made them call the Tarantula too—not calling him that, of course.

"Does any of this look familiar to you, Caroline?" he asked when he arrived, standing first—as appeared to be his way—in the threshold of the sliding metallic door.

She looked around for form at the soft underwater light of the bay, the pods on warehouse racks along the walls, some of them still occupied, and she imagined somewhere on the ship some kind of sleep roster: an organized schedule that dictated shifts of aging or dreaming. They stood before her own pod, which Molly had machine-maneuvered out of the stack, and it sat on its crate, cleaned and empty and unhooked from its bundle of wires and tubes. The number stencil on the side was 23 and meant nothing to her.

"I can't remember if I dreamed. I remember waking with a memory—just the one and nothing more."

"That may be the key to what went wrong," said the Tarantula. "Sleepers are supposed to dream, to keep the mind supple."

"What memory?" Gordon asked, heavy with hope. His eyes constantly pleaded with her to remember, to *think*. She couldn't look at them. They were a rebuke he probably didn't intend.

She looked past the three and down the long arc of the room. It did have an arc, turning, she imagined, with the shape of the ship. She didn't remember this place. It was new to her: every vent and panel and light-emitting diode.

"I was a girl and there were trees around me, and I held out my arm and someone—I don't know who—set a spider on my wrist. It was the size of my hand, and it went slowly up my arm. I could feel its legs tickling, the weight of it and its blackness on my skin. I held my arm straight out forward, and it walked toward me, up my arm, and I could see its asterism set of eyes in parentheses markings in the middle of its head; and also its mouth, like two unformed legs, moving independently. And I remember looking at it and thinking that it had a mind—that it knew certain incomprehensible things—and it was coming to whisper them into my ear so that I would understand."

When she was done, all three of them straightened again from where they had bent forward for her story. Gordon was red around the cheeks. Molly, looking at her, asked what happened next.

"That's all."

"You never told me about that," Gordon said. "Before, when—we were together; you never told me a thing like that. You grew up in Oslo, Caroline. Do you remember? The strange music of that city. Your father worked for the Elevator Embassy there. We met in a lunar training dome; don't you remember that? The time we sat in our suits and watched Earth rise; a picnic with our feet dangling over the edge of a crater. That's what we called it: our picnic. It was so silent but for your voice in my ear, and Earth looked so loud… But that's what you remember? Trees and a spider?"

They'd let him talk, and Molly had rested her hand on Gordon's shoulder, and she tried, for him, to sense that same loss, which she could see in his eyes. She tried with great effort, but all she felt was confusion.

She sensed her own powerful coldness—the frigid distance at which she held herself, and she felt as if she had fallen through the ice that Molly had seen cracking under her and emerged a monster, and she held her own arms because she didn't know these others enough to let them do it.

"Caroline, do you see any spiders now?"

She studied this man, this doctor, whom she'd thought of as the Tarantula, having applied to him a convenient role that she no longer thought him capable of: he had no secrets to whisper into her ear and could not help her remember. She shook her head. "Not here."

"Where then?"

She looked at him.

"I'm willing to indulge you, to a point, Caroline. Where do you think you need—"

"Caroline, you're the captain of the ship; you're the ranking officer!" Gordon screamed suddenly. Molly went for him, but he dodged away and turned smack into the doctor, both of them toppling and Gordon still shouting while they sprawled: "They kept it from you—*oof*! You outrank all of them. You're the captain. Demand all the documents, everything! You're the captain!"

She may have slept—she didn't know. But she was certain that she was awake now and that this was not a dream. She lay still on her back in a pool of viscous fluid in a closed place like a casket. There was a spider on her chest. Standing between the little dunes of her breasts, all eight nubs of contact and all eight eyes. It was still, and so was she, and she looked down the length of her chin, her chest to where it sat gawking in the manner of gas masks. It moved its palps in a jerking motion, a leg on either side of it lifting as if threatened, and she made a monument of her stillness—her breath slow, though it must have had no difficulty determining the condition of her terror, standing as it was with its body-sense and its cruel patience directly above the groundswell of her heart. It moved then. A gradual, leg-lurching ease to where it could caress her chin and then draw its body up into a felt place where it was so close she couldn't fully see it except as a black star hanging over her, demonically unfurled—its terrible weight against the bones of her face as it guided itself ponderously and silently to a level with her ear.

She asked where they'd taken Gordon, and she was told that he was fine, he was watching through the security feed, but that he wouldn't be allowed to twist her condition into a further legal debacle.

"I liked his honesty," she said, wishing that she could have said more for him and certain that she once had. But it seemed that more than her memory was lost.

There were two of them across from her in a matte-metallic room with a wall full of screens and sensors and intermittently blinking lights. They were seated at a table shaped like a nail clipping, and she was on the inside. One of them was the Tarantula, though, now he was just the doctor—longer of hair, though still centrally absent. The other was a man with a queasy smile who told her his name and that they knew each other well and that he was the ship's legal expert, and she nodded politely at him and said nothing.

"Caroline, the issue is that Gordon has made this very complicated for us," said the lawyer. "There are only a few situations in which the secondary command of any ship too distant to communicate with Ground Control can legally cause a captain to step down from his or her post. We woke up the Doc here ahead of schedule because we needed unanimity in order to continue with the termination of your post, but he stipulated—correctly, I believe—that we first needed to see if you were capable of, ah, returning to—a state of—" he looked down at his documents.

"If you could regain your memory," said the doctor.

"Gordon's lack of discretion strung us up in a web," said the lawyer. "Because there's no legal distinction between knowing a thing because you're told and remembering of your own accord—to your position, that is."

"So I can give orders?"

The two men glanced at things, thinking.

She watched the doctor and his calm, ugly features. "If you grant that I have the authority to give an order, then I'd also have the authority to resign."

They looked up. She thought of spider's webs. She thought of the brain scans they had of her in a lab somewhere on this ship called *Travel Light*—her mind translucent to them on screens, undergoing complicated, smoothly-running programs of diagnoses she couldn't begin to understand. She set her hands on the table: cold and pale with blue deltas of veins, and she couldn't remember anything they'd done, these hands. Not much, at least; not back very far. In the cyropod, she had set her thumb against the light of an alarm to hide it, but it had shone straight through her, and that was what she knew.

"I'll make a deal with you," she said. "I get to give one order, and once that's fulfilled, I will admit, on record, to my belief that my memories won't return. And I'll resign." Resign from a post that she didn't know she had with a signature that would be a forgery.

"What order?" asked the lawyer.

"I want to be taken outside. Molly can take me—attach me to a chord or whatever safety procedures she thinks necessary. When we come back in, I'll sign whatever you need me to."

"Ah. Well that's—" the lawyer looked at the doctor. "Doable, I suppose."

"Caroline, why? Can I ask that? Why do you want to go out there? Molly is trained for a space-walk on an accelerating ship. Most of us are not."

Behind her eyes, she could see the blinking light slowing, dimming beneath her thumb where she'd tried to hide from it. She had a powerful sense of time without the attendant memories with which to judge time by, and it was like the chill of a sudden shadow, time was; an absence; it was like a spider's whisper as it crimped itself around the soft flesh of her hearing, chittering prayerlike into that canal of her: could she have translated the chitinous caress into all she had lost? Even if she hadn't panicked anew, set off the alarms? It had only been a dream, perhaps a delusion, crawling along the body's fear-sewn ley lines—warping itself over a cistern newly emptied and rapidly being filled with fear and with shadow.

She knew that the spider had been real in the way that time was real, though she wished it to be otherwise. She wished to stand in a suit on the outside and add whatever it was she saw out there to the few remembrances she had; to see pale light which had forgotten its star in common darkness: the almost-infinite pricks of age unranged and amnesic: memories unmoored and lost. And to hang suspended at the end of a weblike cable and float in that forgottenness; and this would be her one reprieve from the fog that was to be her life now bifurcated by a before and an after, both equally uncertain.

She didn't want to explain this to the doctor who was not the Tarantula. Wanted only to be out there and to look above and below at the cooled-by-distance light and its silent acceptance, knowing that when she returned inside—free and as equally unmoored—that the spider would be there with her. About to whisper into her ear what it remembered.

Andrew Reichard lives in Grand Rapids, Michigan. His short fiction has appeared in journals such as The Collagist, Black Static, Space & Time, Shoreline of Infinity, and others.

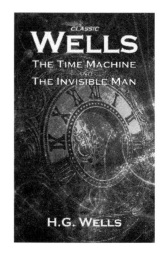

Ask Not

Marion Pitman

A loud discordant bell tolled from a distant tower, and I knew the king was dead. My love was dead. When we were young, we loved as one dreams of loving. If he had been a peasant or a merchant, I should have been his wife. But his great lords would not permit a king to marry a woman with no land, no matter what her powers, and they made him marry a flat-faced woman from the north. She was uncomely, which did not trouble me, but she was dull of mind, and that was a grief to me, that my love should spend his nights with no bright wit to spark his own.

We could, of course, have married with the left hand, and gone on as before, but it seemed to us both that this would devalue both me and the flat-faced wife – whom I did not bear ill-will, it was her misfortune as well as ours.

In time I married an artificer, and we were as happy as anyone has any right to expect. He died two years gone – he was older than I – and I thought of my love, the king, and wondered should we ever meet again. And then I heard the bell that tolled the strokes for the passing of a king, and knew that we should not, in this life. And I knew that I had now a duty to perform.

I am, of course, no longer young. My hair is grey and silver, and I cover it with a gold net. Everything passes, and I was never beautiful, but that is no matter. I still have my wits, and I still have power to conjure, and better judgment now of how to use that power.

When we were young, I and my king, we did a thing that now I think was less than wise – we made a vow. Youth is a time for making vows, but some of them are hard to keep in age. Still, once it is made, it is made, and our aged selves must make the best of it.

When I had heard the bell, and wept, and drunk a glass of wine, I went to my study.

I climbed the library steps to a shelf I had not visited for years, and took down a dusty leather volume. I don't know what creature lost its hide to make the binding, but it was still sound and strong, not crumbling or peeling like cheap calf. I laid it on the desk, and opened it to a page I remembered very well. I looked a long time at the black copper-plate writing, and made a note in my mind of what I would need; then I closed the book and went downstairs.

It wasn't a complicated spell. I had most of the ingredients, and the fresh blood would be my own. I baked a new white loaf, and after some searching found the drawer where I had kept hidden the king's ring, that he gave me when we parted, in the bezel of which was a lock of his hair. He had the same of mine: I wondered what the flat-faced queen would make of that when it was found. Probably nothing – it would go into his treasury with everything else.

I gathered my ingredients and went to the study to wait for dusk.

Of course, the traditional way is to lie on the beloved's grave for a year and a day, but my love would be buried in a great tomb in the cathedral, and if I had tried to lie on it for a day, let alone a year, I would have ended up in a dungeon or a madhouse. So this way it was; I am a wise woman, and I knew the way.

The sun sank blood red in the west, as I fancied I saw the towers of the king's palace black against the sky. I drank the wine, the blood, the burned hair; I broke the loaf and offered it to those whose offering it is. Spirits I could not quite see gazed at me with grief and compassion, but also with reproach and unease. I knew it was a dangerous thing I approached, and probably foolish, but a vow is not to be broken, especially to the dead, and – I was curious. I spoke the words, the words I had known so long, and never let myself think of until now. I lit the candle, and poured one drop of blood on the flame, that disappeared as the flame leaped up. The shuttered windows were black, and behind the flame the air began to glow blood red and flame gold, as out of the blood and wine a face began to rise.

It took all my courage to look into those eyes. They burned and sparked like salt tinder gathered from the beach, blue and green and white as well as gold. Something like lips beneath them moved, and something like a voice spoke.

It said, "Well?"

My mouth was dry and my tongue felt heavy, but I said, "What is the purpose of life? What is the value of love? What is the meaning of death?"

The sound like a voice made a sound like a laugh.

"The purpose of life is love. The value of love is infinite. Death has no meaning."

Then in an instant, the light went out, and I found I had burned my hand.

It was after that that my love, the king, returned.

He appeared not as a misty shadow or a disembodied face, but as a man from head to foot, solid and real. I knew the one thing I must not do was touch him, but it was hard to hold back.

For I don't know how long we stood and gazed at one another, as we had often done in the old days – sometimes it was all we needed. He didn't look as he had when we were young, nor as he must have done when he died, but as a man of forty or so, strong and upright, with just a little grey in his beard.

He said, "You remembered the vow."

"Yes," I said, "I remembered."

"And you're not afraid."

"I'm terrified. But a vow must be kept."

He moved his hand towards me, then quickly took it back. He said, "Sophia," (he always called me Sophia), "it seems there is a reason for this, that we knew not when we made the vow. The boy needs you. Edric needs you."

(The boy, Edric, was not our son. But he was the closest thing we had.)

I said, "The boy has been dead for ten years."

"I know. But – he is trapped. He must be freed to move on. Will you do that?"

"Of course," I said, "but can you not free him?"

"I'm afraid," he said, "that we must both do it. Together. That is how it is. And you must take my hand. You know what that means."

I drew a breath; "I know," I said. "I know. But there – I would have given my life for him while he lived. And I have lived a long life."

"Then take my hand," said the king, "and come with me."

So I took his hand, and at once we were no longer in my study. I cannot say exactly where we were; it seemed to be on fire, but even so there was not much light to see by. There were blood-red shadows everywhere, and I could not see the king so well as I had before. He led me down a flight of steps that

I could not see at all, but had to feel my way with my feet, and we came at last into a tunnel that was entirely dark. He led the way without hesitation, which made me think it was not dark to him, but only to my still living eyes.

At the end of the tunnel was a hall, huge and busy with people; they moved about and spoke to one another, but I heard no sound, and they passed us without a glance, they never saw us. We moved through them till we came to a pair of thrones.

On the right hand throne sat a person dressed in gold and black. Their face was the most beautiful I ever saw, except that there seemed to be no-one inside – that is, no thought or emotion animated it, it was like a mask, a mask made of living flesh. And on the left hand throne sat Edric. He looked a little younger than when he drowned, when his boat was sunk by the sea serpent – a fine, strong boy with muscular arms and copper coloured hair, still in his fisher's smock and canvas trousers. He also did not see us: he was gazing with rapt attention at the person on the other throne, and his gaze did not shift for a moment, though all round him people moved and spoke.

The king said to me, "Sophia, you must distract their attention, while I take the boy. Their beauty has enthralled him, and he cannot see anything else."

"How should I do that?"

He hesitated – "I can't say. But they are alive and so are you. You must be the one to do it."

So I walked up to the throne and called to the beautiful face, "Sire – will you speak to me?" but although I think they heard me, they did not move or speak. Then I laid my hand on their arm, and they turned to me that beautiful mask of a face, and rose, and stepped down from the throne; and the most perfect terror possessed me, that I might not speak or move or cry out; but I stood, and I tried with all my strength to say, "Let him go", but no sound left my lips. All the same, they continued to stand and stare at me, the other living being in this land of the dead, and the emptiness of the eyes in the beautiful face was like the emptiness of hell. And at some point I lost consciousness; my vision turned red and black and I felt myself falling.

The king was kneeling beside me, holding my hands. He said, "Well done, Sophia. The boy is freed to go on. I will take you back."

So I stood, and we went back through the room. I cannot remember whether I looked at the thrones, or if I did, whether there was anyone there. If I saw the person in gold and black again I cannot remember it.

We walked through the tunnel, and up the stairs to the place full of fire, and we stepped out into my study, and my love the king said, "Thank you."

"And now?"

"Now you will go back to your life, and I will see you in a year and a day."

"So be it. Since I have touched you, will it make any difference if I kiss you?"

"It will make no difference."

So we kissed, perhaps the sweetest kiss we ever shared, and then I was alone.

And I am writing this, why? Because I respect knowledge, and the keeping of records, though it is unlikely any will ever read it, and if they do they will not believe it. I have made my will, and seen that everything is as I would wish to leave it. Today it is a year, and tomorrow I will rejoin my love, my king.

Marion Pitman lives outside London, though she would rather live inside it. She has written poetry and fiction most of her life, and published it since the 1970s. She sells second-hand books, and has no car, no cats and no money. Her hobbies include folk-singing, watching cricket, and theological argument. Her short story collection, Music in the Bone, is available from Alchemy Press. www.marionpitman.co.uk

Elevated

Max Sheridan

The Boyles inched closer to each other on the living room sofa and smiled for their seven o'clock photo. Their performance had been well above the ninetieth percentile for most of the month, so when the results flashed across the TV screen and they'd scored just shy of eighty-three, Gerry Boyle was heartbroken.

He double-checked the photo on his mobile just to be sure. Stared at it for a long moment and put the phone back in his pocket. He went to the kitchen and poured out a shot of goji juice. He poured a shot for Megan.

"Zoomi, will you please give us a moment?"

They hadn't powered Zoomi down once since installation, so no one knew what to expect. Even Megan felt a little naked without Zoomi. It was as if the entire house

had shed some critical warmth and vitality. The Natur-L smart spotlights glowed less richly. The Booster Corp spill-free carpet turned the color of spoiled meat. Without Zoomi, the house was just a random conglomeration of manmade materials piled together for basic utility. A skeleton without a nervous system.

The twins left the room on cue. In another minute, the sound of a small finger forcing on a hallway light switch echoed through the dead house.

"We barely hit eighty-three tonight," Gerry said.

"That low?" Megan said.

"You weren't happy."

"I thought I was smiling."

"You weren't."

Gerry Boyle thought for a moment and said, "I'll just tell Zoomi to delete it."

"Can you do that?"

"I don't know."

Gerry joined his wife on the other side of the counter and drew her close. "What's the matter?" he said. "Aren't you feeling elevated?"

Megan peripheraled the counter cam, a smooth white ellipse with a delicate curving white neck that was almost sexual in its need to be touched. The way Gerry was standing now, he was perfectly framed to earn back those seventeen percentage points they'd lost because of her selfishness. A quick selfie with a couple of ear-to-ear smiles would have done it. Though, to be perfectly honest, Megan couldn't really remember if that's the way it worked. If you could swap points from one photo to the next.

"What's the matter?" Gerry said again.

"Nothing," Megan said.

Gerry contemplated the cupboard above the refrigerator where they kept the liquor, a not-so-old habit that felt very old.

"Go ahead," Megan said. "Zoomi isn't watching."

Though Megan wasn't a hundred percent sure of that either. She'd never actually read the whole privacy statement. A paralegal, she should have, but Gerry had assured her that when Zoomi was sleeping, none of their interactions were uploaded to the Elevate Box. No one in Booster Corp's new Dublin headquarters was watching them.

"You want to know the truth?" Gerry said. "I don't want that drink. I don't need it anymore."

"I don't know," Megan said. "I wouldn't mind. Do you really want to feel elevated all the time?"

The sound Gerry made deep in his throat was a silly, high-pitched squeak, but she knew he was serious. "Do I want to feel elevated? You're damn right I want to feel elevated."

"I just mean, maybe I don't want to show it all the time. Maybe I can feel happy and not show it. You know what I mean? Or maybe, I don't know, I don't want to feel elevated all the time."

Gerry filled the tea kettle and activated it. The fact that Zoomi could have done both for him better than he ever could was ironic and further proof of his point. He decided not to dwell on it. Just thinking about the loss of product enjoyment had lowered his mood at least a percentage point. When the tea was done, at whatever temperature the machine had settled on without Zoomi's guidance, he poured himself a green tea and watched it steep.

"Why don't we make love," he said. "That will elevate us."

They'd already reached their weekly performance goal. Four times was a strain on them both. Next month it would climb to five. Friends said that making love five times a week did wonders for your energy levels. You were more or less permanently elevated.

"Sometimes I want to feel like something can still happen," Megan said.

Gerry waited for some new feeling or doubt to emerge, one she hadn't already articulated a hundred times before. But Megan said nothing more, and Gerry knew she wouldn't. They'd been through it all, and they'd both agreed that they weren't in their twenties anymore and that routine was a good thing, a stabilizing thing, the only real way of achieving long-term security and happiness, which was the beating heart of the Elevate Box and the reason why, out of 100,000 Booster Corp employees worldwide, Gerry was one of a thousand chosen to test it.

"Be blue," Gerry smiled, sipping his tea. "Just not in front of the camera at seven o'clock. Zoomi, are you there?"

"Good evening, Gerry."

"Please turn on the wall light in the bedroom. Dim it to two."

It was the cheesiest thing. The fact that they were standing at the Whole Foods cheese refrigerator together only made it worse. Or better. But they both started laughing at the same time when they realized they were looking for the same item on their Yummlies and neither had any idea what it was. Megan deactivated her projector first and said to the man, "I saw that horrible little English chef put it on his pizza. I have no idea why I'm even trying it."

"You're trying it because Zoomi watched you watching it," the man said.

Megan's smile died.

The man said, "You must be beta testing Elevate. So am I."

Megan studied his face, trying to figure out what position he would likely have had at Booster Corp. As much as she hated Zoomi—yes, she hated Zoomi, she might as well admit it—she could have used the AI assistance now, because the only thing she could focus on were the man's full lips and almond-shaped, hazel-colored eyes, the soothing scent of his skin and his firm, white hands.

"My wife was selected," he said finally. "I don't work there."

It was the right thing for him to say, the honest thing, but, still, the words crushed Megan in a way she found almost pathetic. She went back to the cheese shelves, looking for the gourmet Italian cheese they'd both seen on Chef Ross Tweever's cooking program.

"Burrata," the man said.

"What?"

"The cheese we're looking for."

"Yes, that's right," she said. "It's a funny name, isn't it?"

"Ross Tweever is funnier."

"Tweever couldn't be his real name. And this doesn't sound like a real cheese."

"What does real cheese sound like?" the man said.

The burrata was ten dollars, a tiny overpriced blob of designer mozzarella. Megan put one in her basket and offered the man one.

"Emmental," she said. "That's what a real cheese sounds like."

The man's lips smiled.

"I haven't cooked in a while actually," Megan said.

"It's funny," the man said. "I can't even remember when I stopped either. My name's Martin, by the way." He took the cheese from her. The sides of their fingers touched. "You don't work for Booster Corp either," he said.

"What makes you so sure?"

"You wouldn't be shopping. You'd have ordered everything with Baggit. Everyone at Booster Corp does."

It was true, Gerry couldn't understand why she still wasted time at the Whole Foods. It was maybe why she didn't notice the scent of his skin anymore. Had forgotten what his lower lip looked and tasted like.

"I need to get home," she said.

They walked to the register together. Megan felt the flush of her desire in her pores, a delicious aching that made her feel almost light-headed. She barely made it past the checkbot. When the doors sucked them back into the eternal temperateness of the biosphere, Megan's blood was a sweet drumbeat in her ears.

They made love in Martin's Booster coup as it drove them out of the suburbs and onto a one-lane country road that skirted the biosphere. There wasn't much room on the leather back seat. Martin was tall and broad-shouldered. His physical body loomed over her, but when he was inside her, it was as if she was being filled by a gentle feathery static. The tension drained from her body. Soon Megan couldn't feel her legs and the static was pushing against the walls of her belly.

She realized, as she lay panting in the backseat of a complete stranger's car, that it was the first time she'd been satisfied in over a year. And now it was all over. All she could think of the whole way back to the supermarket was how being this elevated couldn't protect her from the terrible loss that was coming when Martin left her in the parking lot and drove away. The thought made her nauseous, giddy and unbelievably happy at the same time.

They reached the supermarket parking lot at six-thirty on the dot. They'd been gone for an hour. When Megan realized just how late it was, her mind spiraled back to reality.

"The photo."

Martin made sure Megan's buttons were all closed. He checked for abrasions on her lips and neck and behind her ears because he hadn't shaved that morning. He found nothing that a Booster Corp line coder would be likely to notice.

"You've done this before," Megan said. She didn't know him at all, so she shouldn't have even cared. Why wouldn't he have done this before? At the same time, it seemed unfair that they would have to stop. Why couldn't they do it again? Have the coup drive them for a few more hours while he made love to her? Drive them out of town even? Drive them forever?

That night the Boyles scored an easy hundred percent elevation and the twins were allowed to watch Elevate Kids News until eight. Megan's cheeks were still hot from lovemaking as Gerry spoke excitedly about the next steps at work. He wasn't sure what they would actually win if they broke the ninety-fifth percentile, but it would likely include new upgrades for Zoomi that they couldn't even imagine.

The kids brushed their teeth and went up to bed and Zoomi told them a story. Downstairs, Gerry turned on *The Lark*. When he recognized the episode, he got up to put a leftover slice of pizza in the microwave.

Zoomi began to cook it.

"We haven't seen this one before," Megan said, squinting at the screen.

"You're right," Gerry said. "But you're still squinting. You should use that clear screen extension I boosted you." Gerry opened the microwave and pulled out his plate. His lips closed over the perfectly reheated burrata.

On the TV, the Booster couple on *The Lark*, who lived in a suburb just like theirs, decided to leave their jobs at Booster Corp and become property agents for a day. There was something tedious about the whole premise of the show, Megan found. No one ever accepted the lark and gave up their job. But that didn't stop her from hoping against all odds that one day a couple would actually decide to throw everything away to farm mullet in the Florida Keys.

"Wonderful burrata," Gerry said.

Megan's heart jack-hammered. *The Lark* went to a final u-mmercial. It felt like a solid minute before the ad came on and the Boyles saw themselves in a set of discounted Boden winter outfits.

"What did you say?" Megan said.

"The name of the cheese," Gerry said. "The one that melts in the center of the pizza."

"Burrata."

"That's what I said."

That night, while Gerry slept, Megan stared at the dark ceiling trying to will a dream of Martin into existence. She pictured him somewhere else. At the liquor store. It was a cozy night for two with a bottle of Spanish red and a rom-com. They fed each other lo mein on Martin's couch, her legs nesting on Martin's lap under a crocheted quilt. It was chilly out because in Megan's fantasy the coders at Booster Corp, who had no sense of style and preferred to go around in T-shirts year round, didn't control the biosphere's temperature.

She fast-forwarded the daydream to the end of the crappy Sandra Bullock movie they were watching. When the credits started to unspool on the TV, her hand slipped beneath the sheet and reached for anything Martin had left behind.

The next afternoon Megan was at the Whole Foods café at four o'clock. Gerry often came home early, but four was a reasonable hour for her to be out. Zoomi would let the kids in and prepare their snacks. She would help them with their homework.

Megan sipped a dark French roast, wondering if you could check into a hotel at four in the afternoon, not knowing if Martin would even show.

Martin showed at fifteen past. Zeroed right in on her table.

They left in Megan's Prius.

The idea of making love in a paid room was so Hollywood it felt exhilarating, even if Megan had been looking forward to something more spontaneous and challenging. Stretched out on the hotel sheets, filled by Martin, she realized all their friends had missed the point. Making love to a man you're deliriously attracted to once is all you needed to stay elevated for a week.

They stayed in bed for an hour. Martin got up first. Megan watched Martin curled over his boots at the edge of the bed, his pale torso etched in muscle and rib. Even his back was attractive.

Megan said, "I wonder if we were married we'd be fucking around on each other."

Martin peripheraled her.

"You shouldn't say things like that."

"Why not?"

"Because they're true. You'd hate my breath and find me boring. You'd be staring at the ceiling at night dreaming of someone else. You have no idea what I even do."

"And I'm not going to ask. I actually do stare at the ceiling dreaming of you. You're perfect."

"I'm an assassin."

"A pitiless one, I'm sure."

"I sell auto insurance."

"Never." She pressed her toe against his back. "What if we were meant to be together, Martin? What if that was our elevation?"

Martin was all dressed now. He stood, then sat back down next to Megan's naked body. Her breasts were still warm, her flesh pliant and flushed. She wondered if she could get him to undress again.

"I mean it," Megan said. "Why don't we pretend we're on *The Lark*, but actually do something about it."

"Quit our jobs?"

"Our miserable lives."

"Who told you I was miserable?" He kissed her on the forehead and felt around in his jacket pocket for his mobile and incogged the room using a Booster alias account so when the payment went through, the hotel room wouldn't start showing up in his u-mmercials.

She said, "In *Pretty Woman*, they ordered room service." She saw herself on the couch with Martin watching Julia Roberts and Richard Gere living happily after ever, wondering what Martin's lips would taste like if he'd been eating lo mein.

"I've never seen that one," he said.

"*Pretty Woman*? You've got to be kidding me."

He studied her, but not as if he was trying to recall the memory of a film. It was something else. For the first time, Martin's gaze unnerved Megan. Before she could arrange an appointment for tomorrow, he was gone as perfectly as he'd come.

That evening the Elevate Box surprised them with a highlight slideshow. In each of the fourteen photos the box chose, the Boyles were smiling effortlessly, but towards the end of the slideshow there was something else, something radiant, and it was Megan.

Gerry Boyle quickly did the math. With the new data, he expected they'd eclipsed their monthly goal by a good two percentage points.

"I mean, we can't be sure," he told Megan once the kids were in bed and they were alone in the living room. "There's an algorithm behind it. But if you're not smiling in one photo, and Elevate suspects it was an anomaly, there's a good chance it will weigh it down."

"Almost like deleting it," Megan said.

"Almost. I've got to run to the office for a minute."

While she wasn't going to miss Gerry, she'd still grown used to having him on the couch next to her at night while they watched *The Lark*.

Gerry slipped into his scooter scrubs.

"Need anything while I'm out?" he said.

The idea that Gerry would stop by a brick-and-mortar and bring her something back might have been the most romantic gesture he'd made in years. It made Megan feel like she was seven again and could choose whatever she wanted from the Amazon truck, a toy or a piece of candy or a new pen. But he obviously didn't mean that at all. He meant he'd have Zoomi send the order to Baggit.

"I'm fine," she said, and opened *Pretty Woman* on the Elevate Box.

She tried to watch, but the film didn't make any sense to her anymore. She'd always liked Richard Gere for reasons she'd never been able to articulate. Tonight he did nothing for her. She needed Martin. She could be forgiven for not asking for Martin's details. He made her delirious. She couldn't concentrate on anything but his sex when they were together. But why hadn't he asked for hers? He'd found her up to now, but that was only because they'd shown up at the same time. What if she'd gotten to the Whole Foods at three o'clock and not four?

She went upstairs and slipped out of her yogas and pulled the covers up to her neck as if it were a cold November night and she needed the extra warmth. But her toes were warm and you couldn't pretend to be cold if your toes were warm.

She watched the ceiling and played her own version of *Pretty Woman* where she was taking Julia Roberts' bubble bath. Instead of waiting for Martin to take his shoes off at the very end, and feel the warm, live grass blades sliding between his naked toes, she put him in the bathtub with her. She curled up in Martin's brick-and-mortar lap.

"Turn the lights off, Zoomi."

Zoomi did nothing.

Megan said, "Zoomi, will you please turn off the lights?"

The lights stayed on.

Megan heard noises downstairs. She thought of the children first, but the command to lock them safely in their rooms froze on her lips. Ironically, her next thought was of Martin. What if the night intruder was her lover, come to her because he couldn't sleep either, his chestnut hair plastered with rain, the coup purring in the driveway, ready to take her away forever.

But it was just Gerry. Despite the sound-dampening Booster Corp carpet, she could practically feel his chunky thighs plodding up the stairs.

Megan drew the covers down from her neck and picked up a paperback novel from the night table and opened up randomly to a page she'd read before.

Gerry came in sweaty.

"Scooter break down?" Megan asked.

"Out of juice," Gerry said. He peripheraled the paperback in Megan's hands. "Thought you'd finished that one."

"I probably have. Twice. I can't ever remember where I stopped."

"Which is why you should be using Booster Flip," Gerry said. "Flip always knows where you've stopped and always opens up to the right place."

"I like real books. Anyway, paper puts me to sleep."

"Which is the point of reading?"

"What did you need at the office?"

Gerry slipped out of his sweats and hopped into bed naked. It excited Megan strangely. Gerry smelled better sweaty than he did bathed.

"Forgot to share a corp folder with Burroughs," he said. "He'll need it tomorrow for the Boost."

"Big day?"

"Well, now that you ask."

Gerry told Megan about the latest developments in the Booster AI program. He wasn't really involved in it, but news was trickling in through the grapevine. Mainly through Burroughs. Once the specs went to marketing, and word got out, Gerry expected the buzz would shatter records.

"Sounds exciting," Megan said.

"They're already in beta," Gerry said.

Megan peripheraled Gerry. Moved a little closer to his warm, sweaty body.

"In the biosphere? Doing what?"

"Anything you can do, but better."

"I don't think I really understand what that would mean."

But she did, or thought she did. She rolled back over onto her side of the bed and watched the wall, wishing she didn't. She would have asked why. But what was the reason for any of it? For Zoomi? For the Elevate Box itself?

Of course, men like Burroughs would be gloating over what they'd done. Selling corporate on the idea that you couldn't even tell them apart. But she knew that wasn't true. You could tell them apart.

They were too perfect. Smelt too nice. Made love too well. Always said the right thing. Found you no matter where you were. It was awful, but she wanted to tell Gerry everything. Booster Corp had actually failed. Life wasn't perfect. You couldn't feel elevated a hundred percent of the time, and you wouldn't want to. Perfect only worked in movies.

She turned back over.

Gerry was already playing a dream extension. Megan couldn't see Gerry's face, but she knew he was smiling wide as he entered an Amazon encampment and prepared for his welcome bath or led the first human mission to the Rim Planets only to discover they were already populated by an advanced civilization of sexy, purple women.

Megan turned to the night table and shut off the lights herself.

It was Martin who was waiting at the Whole Foods today. He wore a fawn-colored sports coat over a white button-down shirt. Megan had come in her yogas. They took Megan's Prius again.

Megan deactivated self-drive and drove out of the biosphere and towards the mountains on a road she vaguely remembered from her childhood. She was unhappy that even outside the biosphere the temperature hadn't dropped. She wanted to feel the need to wrap herself around Martin.

Martin said nothing when they left the biosphere and began to see their first non-Booster Corp habitations, then gas stations and ammo shops. When they stopped for gas and put the town of Junction behind them, he said, "You didn't even incog it."

"So what," Megan said.

The first picnic site came and went. They wound further into the mountains. The air never cooled. Megan peripheraled the bottle of Maker's Mark on the floor behind Martin's seat. That was all the proof Gerry would need, not some shitty motel in the mountains ending up on her Boost feed.

They came to the turn-off for Buffalo Rock, which Megan also remembered from before Booster Corp. There was a boulder shaped like a bison's head overlooking an endless treescape. As a child, she'd sat on its massive flat yellow head sunning herself like a cat. The days before the vast regularity. Days of dirtiness and insecurity. When the sun dropped at Buffalo Rock back then, you felt it. They parked in a picnic area and walked for fifteen minutes along a marked but unused path until they reached the edge of the woods.

Buffalo Rock wasn't as big as Megan remembered it. Not as yellow, not as hot. There was no one else about. Megan sat on the edge of the rock and pulled off her driving scrubs. She let her feet hang over treetops that in the mid-November air still maintained a succulent greenness. She held the bottle of bourbon by its neck.

Her instinct told her to peripheral her surroundings for the unblinking white eye of a hidden forest cam. Maybe Booster Corp had claimed more of the world than just the biosphere. How would you know? Would you even care at this point?

She studied Martin, trying to re-experience the handsomeness of his face, the beauty of his body for the first time. How, she wondered, would you code a face and body like that into existence? She ran her hand over the smooth glass neck, realizing she didn't even know how you made a bottle.

A flesh-and-blood noise pulled her away from her thoughts.

A family had stepped out of the woods behind them, a mother and father and two young children. They were locals, possibly from Junction or further up in the mountains. Their complexions were waxy and bloated from the preservative-rich, nutrient-poor food they bought at the brick-and-mortars. If they'd ever smiled in their lives, this was as distant a memory as good, healthy food. Oddly, they were unarmed, carrying only paper sacks for foraging.

Booster Corp had told them again and again that humans on the other side were always armed. That accidents outside the Booster Corp's 156 domed communities in the continental United States weren't covered by any Booster Corp health insurance policies, and of course they would know if you'd been outside.

Megan wanted to offer the family some food, good, organic food. But the family disappeared back into the woods as uneventfully as it had appeared before she could even say hello.

"The poor children," Megan said. "We did this to them."

Martin said nothing. Megan sipped off the bourbon.

"Did you hear me?" Megan said. "We destroyed what we had and we left them the broken pieces. And now we're doing it all over again with the Elevate Box. One of these days, I'll be out here with a paper bag just like them." She pressed the bottle on Martin, wondering if he even knew what it was.

"But not you," she said. "You'll always have a home in Booster Corp."

"Are you feeling ok?" Martin said.

Megan turned to face Martin. In the rich late afternoon light, Martin's ears, the inner ears, were completely, intricately hairless.

"How did you find me, Martin?" Megan said. "You were at the cheese refrigerator at the same time. You were at the cafe at the same time. You fucked like clockwork. Beautifully, but like clockwork." And you've never seen *Pretty Woman*, she thought. Never fallen in love with Julia Roberts falling in love with Richard Gere.

"When I was a kid we'd come to places like Buffalo Rock and make pacts we'd keep for life," Megan said. "Did they give you a memory of that, Martin? We'd cut our fingers and mash them together so our blood mixed."

That fact that Martin didn't, or couldn't, respond was actually a relief. Instead, Megan noticed an odor. Was it some artificial fear response making his skin turn? Or pheromones? Had Martin been programmed by Booster Corp, like millenia of carbon-made men before him, to find angry women erotic?

If that was the case, Megan felt sad for them both.

"If you were real," she said, "this would hurt."

Almost without thinking, she shattered the bottle of bourbon against the edge of the cliff. The jagged bottleneck was like a primitive glass dagger. She scraped at Martin's shoulder with it. A thick line of blood oozed out of the wound. In seconds it was trickling freely.

"Oh, my God," Megan said. "You're real."

"What the fuck?" Martin said. He said it over and over again, until he said, "You cut me."

"I didn't mean to," Megan said.

"But you did. You fucking cut me."

"I thought—" But how to explain it? And what if—well, what if they were simply programmed to bleed? If Martin was a bot and she told Gerry, would Gerry even care? Would it be ok if she was screwing a bot?

Gerry screwing purple space women in his dreams was one thing. But if she was fucking AI, then what would be the point? Of anything?

Why wouldn't the temperature just drop? Twenty years ago, you dove into ice cold water and you sunned yourself on hot rocks. A kiss was tongues and nerve endings. Making love was real, not a goddamn video game. She wanted Martin more than anything, and now that she had him, she'd lost him and she didn't know what to do next.

Martin was already heading for the tree line at a trot, waving down the family. His long, lithe body looked funny this way, almost as funny as Gerry's squeaky voice when it got caught in his throat.

Below Megan's feet, the trees murmured in the breeze. Her yogas were damp with bourbon. She knew she could do it. She could make Gerry more spontaneous, if that's what it took. She could make him more attentive to her needs. She could, in theory, have everything she had with Martin with Gerry.

On her way back to the biosphere Megan combed the first few gas stations for signs of Martin's fawn-colored blazer or a fresh trail of his blood on the pavement. Then she stopped looking and set the Prius to self-drive. She leaned back and listened to herself breathing.

A few minutes after she crossed back into the biosphere, an incoming call flashed across the dashboard. The worst scenarios ran through Megan's head.

She'd been caught on camera slicing Martin's shoulder.

Zoomi had burnt the house down by accident while preparing toast for the kids.

The biosphere actually didn't exist. It was all a dream and they were sleeping.

But it was only Gerry, and he was very happy.

Booster Corp had published their monthly Elevate Box performance quotas.

They'd made the ninety-ninth percentile.

*Max Sheridan is the author of **Dillo** (Shotgun Honey Press, 2018) and a few other stories. He lives and writes in*

Fixed Line
Denali Stannard

The radio coughed out dead air and a voice that said, "Lost him. Going back for- Lost. Can't feel- Lost. Lost."

It had been saying that for the past half an hour, and Cal nudged the frequency a little to make it stop. It was nothing she wasn't used to, but she was tightly wound, alone in the tent, with only the dull thud of ropes slapping nylon to keep her company.

It couldn't hurt to check in, even though the party was likely well out of range and they hadn't responded to her for over an hour.

"Buster crew, this is Dr. Bridges from Camp Three. Checking in on your status, over."

Static but no voices; not Iumo's deep rumble or Rio's sharp cackle. Cal tried again, willing the transmission up the icefall, through the maze of crevasses and frayed rope.

"Busters, this is Bridges. It's just me and the ghost in the machine down here, you gotta give me something. Maybe a pity laugh for the joke?" Cal discovered she was laughing herself, a little hysterically. Not a good look on a public frequency. "Um. Over."

"Over," said the radio, a man's voice.

Cal's thumb turned white as she jabbed it down on the push-to-talk button. "Iumo?"

"Over," said the radio, thin and childlike now. "Over? Over! Over!" There was a chorus of voices, singing, moaning, screaming. There was the crash of ice and the groan of wind, and the crowding voices of the dead.

Cal left the radio in the corner and burrowed into her sleeping bag, trying to ignore the tapping against the tent walls; trying not to picture fingers, black-tipped, burnt with cold.

If the party up on the serac had anything to say about it, the voices would be gone come dawn.

That's why you hired exorcists, after all.

The corpses had been piling up on Neverfall for years. There were slopes and ridges where the snow was dotted with the parkas and down suits of the dead. Someone should do something, said opinion pieces and families who bridled at their loved ones reduced to macabre landmarks. 'Turn left at the skeleton in the yellow jacket taking a breather against a rock. That's Sharit Walker, his kids were in the papers the other week, begging for someone to bring him home.'

But the mountain kept what you gave her, and there was no chipping a body free of half a ton of ice and shale, then carrying the frozen weight of it to basecamp. Not when it was five miles down in air so thin you might as well be breathing vacuum, ribs cracked from your coughing and your blood thick as slurry.

And if the bodies were bad, the ghosts were worse.

They flapped in the wind, bright and ragged as prayer flags. Scraps of Gore-Tex and leather hung on frames of bone and memory; faces swollen, frost-scared blurs. Sometimes they stayed where they died, wailing and babbling, replaying their final gasping moments. Sometimes they followed climbers from base camp to summit, or clustered around pitched tents, pressing against the fly.

It was horrible. It was a safety hazard. Their whisperings choked the airwaves, making it harder and harder to tell the frantic call of an injured climber from the echoes of an accident of thirty years before.

"It's the responsible thing to do," Rio had said when the papers asked her why she was spearheading the Neverfall Cleansing Campaign.

Responsibility nothing. Rio Varga had the same instinct for publicity that cats had for mice, the same habit of leaving torn up press clippings on their bed. Rio climbed like a cat too, lithe and graceful, leaping from hold to precarious hold, teeth and tawny hair flashing in sunlight unfiltered by atmosphere.

Rio had drummed up thousands of dollars in supplies and sponsorships, and two of the valley's fittest exorcists swathed in prayer beads and down jackets. And now here they were, on an expedition to the peak of the tallest mountain in the world.

Here Cal was, waking in the dark to the radio popping and whispering.

"Cal," came Rio's voice, in the snow-soft murmur she saved for when it was just them. "Where are you? *Cal*."

That was all that came through. Cal threw herself from her sleeping bag and sat freezing in her thermal underwear trying to get her back.

By morning, the radio was still dead. It hadn't said another word - not in Rio's voice, not in Iumo's, not in anyone's - and that scared Cal more than any choir of ghosts.

The team was supposed to check in when they made it to alpine Camp Four. They were supposed to make it there by 1700. By 0400, they still hadn't checked in.

And Dr. Cal Bridges had hit her limit.

"I've been up there before," Cal told the blue-cloaked skybride. The woman was a devotee of Neverfall, the mountain climbers nicknamed the Bride and courted just as fervently. Blasphemously, if you minded what the skybrides said about the sanctity of the mountain goddess's snow.

Cal didn't ask what this priestess was doing at Camp Three, or mention that on her last attempt Cal had turned back two hundred meters from the summit. "And the Pike last year. I know what I'm doing. I won't slow you down."

The priestess looked doubtful. When you were twitchy, bespectacled, and ninety pounds in your crampons, people made assumptions about your climbing ability, but at least this woman looked like she'd hold Cal in equally low regard if she was six two and built like a linebacker.

"We want the same thing. It makes sense to pool resources."

"I want you the fuck off this mountain," said the priestess. She was half a foot taller than Cal, imposing in a blue snowsuit and iron spiked boots.

"I'm sorry?"

"I want you off my mountain," she repeated. "You, your friends, their bodies, their ghosts. I want your garbage gone, your shit scoured from my lady's flanks. I want all of you, living or dead, off my *fucking* mountain."

Cal remembered suddenly why this woman looked so familiar; she'd been the spokesperson during the May season, two years ago, when a whole expedition had gone missing.

"We told them not to come here," she'd told reporters who'd come looking for rustic prayers for lost souls. "*Everything* told them not to come here, from the blood thickening in their veins to the rising waters in their lungs. Stop sending your fools here to die. We can't hear ourselves think for their babble in the night."

There had been a stink about it. Reams of commentary on the bitter locals who hadn't turned enough profit on the ascension industry and resented the success of those who had. Rio had read it to Cal over breakfast.

"Okay," said Cal, hooking her mittened thumbs into her pack straps and staring up at the woman who carried an ice axe like a crozier and disdain like a miter. "Fair enough. But I'm not turning back. My crew is up there. My friends, my -" Not her girlfriend, not after the night at Camp Two, with the thrown cook pot, with Cal's furious tears and Rio's exasperated shouts. "-my

friends are up there." Her *only* friends, because Cal didn't make friends easily, and the ones she had were the crazies who threw themselves at the roof of the sky to see if they'd stick. Her friends were big Iumo, whose family talked about him as if he were already dead, and the Laskor twins, who had short-roped each other up Hiluae'a and lost four fingers between them; and yes, Rio, who had broken Cal's heart a dozen times over and who Cal was not about to let vanish without answering for it. "There's a crew up there freezing on the col, and if we let them die, it will be half a dozen new ghosts keeping you up."

"Half a dozen and one," the priestess muttered, breaking eye contact to look Cal up and down. "Fine. Let's go."

It came as an honest shock. Cal had been asking around all morning and everyone she'd approached had pointed to the storm that'd rolled in the night before and was looking to come back around. They'd pointed out that Rio's group were likely safe at Camp Four and hadn't called it in, so going up after them was pointless. Or else they hadn't made it to camp, and going after them was even more pointless.

The woman was already walking away, through the tents of Camp Three towards the ice face that was their pathway to the heights. Her strides were long and Cal hurried to keep pace. The priestess walked like a boulder tumbled, like her arrival was utterly inevitable and her goddess help anyone that tried to stop it. "Let me know when you're ready," the priestess said, spinning open a carabiner at her waist.

"What should I call you?" asked Cal. Being roped to the woman impressed upon her, like it hadn't before, that it was the two of them against the mountain and its secrets; the skybride her only defense against a fall from the heights. "I can't go up on a rope by someone whose name I don't know."

"Anja," said the skybride, and anchored Cal for her climb.

Cal had brought the handheld radio with her and she flicked it on and off as they picked their way up the icefall. Around them, seracs groaned and sweated in the sun, sparkling like the fanciful ramparts of a glass castle.

The first ghost was waiting at the top.

It was an old one, in wool and leather. As Cal flexed her fingers in their gloves and stamped her feet to keep warm, it shuffled closer and closer. By the time Anja hauled herself onto the ledge, huffing in huge lungfuls of meager air, it was almost pressed against Cal's side, stinking of mildew and meat shriveling in the sun.

"Help." Its voice was wind whistling through rocks. "Help. Help me. Help."

Cal tilted her body away from the shadowy bone and sinew, like she did with creeps on the train in the city. "Anja. Can you help it? Please?"

Hunched over, arms braced against her legs, Anja grinned between pants for breath. "Exorcise it? Easily."

"Because," And this had been bothering her for a while. "If you *can*, why haven't you done it before?"

"You and Varga spoke to our Reverend Mother, didn't you?" Anja's raised eyebrow said that she knew that they had, and knew exactly what the Reverend Mother had said; something similar to Anja, minus the cussing. "Evey climber hurts her, even us. You can climb fast and take smoke baths and mouth the right prayers, but a trespass is a trespass. Pain is pain, however sorry you are for causing it."

"But you're up here." Up here with a fall of two hundred feet behind them and something fifty years dead at their side.

"You're a doctor." Anja gestured at Cal and the tattoos on the backs of her hands, under her gloves, that mapped out her profession. "You know that cutting out a tumor means pain. Sometimes the end justifies the means. The Reverend Mother doesn't think so. I do."

Cal had amputated too many gangrenous, black-nailed fingers and toes to disagree. "So you're a heretic?"

"No. I just don't have the patience for bitching and moaning when there's something I can *do*. Speaking of - " She clasped her mitten in her teeth and drew it off, then went rummaging in another pocket for yak knucklebones strung on a thong and a sprig of something resinous. "Set this on fire, would you?"

The flames, when they caught, threw up a fitful plume of smoke, snatched into ribbons by the wind. Cal hunkered over, shielding it as Anja rattled the knucklebones and straightened up to her full height.

This high, the magic caught easier than the fire had. Cal had seen enough exorcisms at the hospital that they'd become as mundane as sending biowaste to the incinerator, but here there was no slow leech of light and life as the spell took hold. The world tipped from color to the charcoal daubs of the Other Place so quickly that Cal almost dropped the sprig, wheezing like she'd been punched.

There was no mountain here, only a black plain beneath a midnight sky. Anja was as solid as ever, the shadows sliding across her round, indifferent face. Before them was the ghost, wrapped in frayed ropes and the ragged remains of a face.

"Help," it said.

"That's why we're here," said Anja, surprisingly soft. "Tell us what happened."

Deaths at the hospital were usually easy. Old or sick or both, with time enough to make some kind of peace before the end. The ones that died beneath the scalpel on operating tables, or came in mangled from accidents and past the point of saving, those needed the coaxing of a priest.

But the ghosts of Neverfall were another matter. You didn't climb her if you didn't want it so badly that you were willing to die for it. And that, ironically enough, made for ghosts that couldn't accept it.

"Help?" said the ghost again.

"We're here to help," said Anja. "Tell me what went wrong."

The ghost was only shadow and despair, so it caught Cal off guard when it said, quite clearly, "Djeri went ahead, when the storm came up. Whiteout."

Cal recognized the cadence of a climbing tale; like any one of her friends telling the story of that one bad spring, that gulch with the bad snow, that time Billie nearly lost an eye in the backcountry.

She hunkered down on her heels like she did when listening to a good disaster, training her ear to the part of the story where she could say 'there's where it went wrong' and avoid repeating it herself one day. "Were you roped together?"

"Whiteout," repeated the ghost. Ragged hands waved at the torn ropes encircling it. This place, on the other side of death, was mutable in the way the world was not. As the ghost spoke, fat white flakes began to fall, soft and textureless as ash. Faster and faster, piling around their ankles until Cal could barely see Anja beside her, and the ghost was only a silhouette against the storm. "I was moving too slow. Lungs. *Hurt*." It let out a keening noise. "I can't keep up, wait up - I'm going to take a breather, let me take a rest… I'm running low… Djeri, I can't see you… Help, help, help…" It dissolved into wails again, swaying where it stood.

"What's your name, bud?" Cal had helped countless raving climbers, delirious with cold and infection and fluid in the brain. She'd held the hands of a hundred frightened patients so deep in shock they couldn't tell her where the bullet had gone in.

It was amazing how a name could anchor you in all that pain. Sometimes it was the only thing you could hold onto.

"You're not alone," Anja added. "We'll help you down. What's your name, honey?"

The whisper floated on the cold air. Cal held it in her mind, and Anja caught it on her knucklebones and held it to the flame.

She spoke the name into the flickering heat and held out her hand. The ghost moved towards her, a shadow reaching -

When its fingertips met the flame, it sighed. And was gone.

Anja blew out the herbs. As the scent faded and the smoke blew away, they were back on the mountainside. There was ash on the ground, and an old, frayed rope.

"Rest in peace," said Cal, inadequately.

"Remain there," said Anja, and beckoned Cal up the crag.

One down, several hundred to go.

The storm came from nowhere.

"Don't you pass out on me," Anja warned. "I'm not saying I couldn't carry you-"

"My twelve-year-old niece can carry me," Cal mumbled. And she had, one time when Cal was babysitting and Ruby had gotten annoyed with her strictures on screen time.

"I have no interest in hauling a flatlander's ass down my lady's flanks, you hear? If you faint, you're still responsible for getting your jackrabbit butt back to base." As Anja chided, her hand was on the small of Cal's back, bracing her against the wind. The security of it allowed Cal to take a few steps. She leaned forward, braced her weight on her ice axe, and somehow found her rhythm again.

Anja's hand patted her lightly between the shoulder blades and then was gone.

Rio's hands had been large and strong too, but always cold. She'd hefted Cal up more cliff faces than Cal could count; braced her on snow bridges until she found her balance; reached out in the dark of their tent to cup Cal's face in a calloused palm. The skin of her fingertips was always rough, her skin dry and cool. She could pull up her own body weight on nothing more than those fingertips, tipping herself up rock faces on the sea stacks back home. She could pull Cal to her, too, and did.

But there was no touch now, cold or otherwise.

Cal turned her face into the wind and let it freeze her tears. The world narrowed to the snow beneath her feet, the rise and fall of her ice-clotted boots and the ache in her lungs.

She almost stumbled into Anja's back. And then, staggering past, almost stumbled over the body slumped on the trail.

There weren't any known dead on this ridge, and for a moment Cal panicked, wondering how far they'd gone off course. But then it stirred.

It was Iumo, face down upon the ice.

Anja was already on her knees, rolling him over. There was an overhang ten feet away, and if they could get him into its shelter it might save him. But Iumo was a big man and up here ten feet might as well be ten miles. Anja strained, grabbing under his armpits and heaving until the veins stood out upon her temples. He slid about a foot.

"He'll have to walk," Cal said, crouching. "Iumo! Hey, buddy, what are you doing lying around up here?" Behind his frosted-over goggles, Iumo's eyelids fluttered. His pulse was weak and very slow and one of his gloves was off, half-buried beside him. Too late, almost certainly, but she eased it back onto his hand, over fingers cold and stiff as chicken straight from the freezer. Frostbite was a problem for if he survived. "*Iumo*, wake up. I've got a skybride here, don't go cluttering up her mountain right in front of her."

Iumo blinked again and his dark eyes focused on her face. Iumo, who'd helped her move into her last apartment, who came to her for advice on asking out the cute girl at the library, and who, after her last fight with Rio, had dropped a heavy hand on her shoulder and said there was no shame in walking away. His lips formed her name without sound and Cal smiled encouragingly. It would be easy to panic, but she'd been doing this a long time. She was almost as practiced at losing friends as she was at saving lives.

"Cal?" he said, slurring the name.

"That's right. Come on, we can't drag your ass so you're gonna have to walk." He had half a tank of oxygen left, though the valve had frozen over. She pounded it free, turned the gas on a notch and strapped the mask in place. "Breathe, Iumo. Let's walk."

With her and Anja's help - mostly Anja's - they got him upright and staggering the ten feet into the cave. They wrapped him in a bag while Anja poured a thermos of syrupy tea down his throat and Cal radioed for help.

"They're sending two traversairs up for you," Cal told him, relieved to see he was starting to shiver. "What the hell happened up there? Why didn't you make it to Camp Four?"

"HAPE," Iumo said. His teeth clacked, and Cal's heart sank. High altitude pulmonary edema was the mountain's favorite killer. "It got one of the exorcist kids. Rio went up with Hachi and the other one, while Hani and I tried to get her down to Camp Three. Then the storm blew in. Lost them in it."

"Rio went up?" Acid seared Cal's stomach; fear, but also anger. "She left you?"

"Gotta finish the job," mumbled Iumo. "Left us with an extra canister of O_2. Hers. Said she'd summited before without gas, so it was no big."

Cal sat back on her heels, fighting panic. Yes, Rio had climbed twice and summited once without oxygen. But less oxygen meant you moved and thought slower, and delusions grew fast. A wise climber would never guide without it, not when other lives depended on the decisions you made and the steps you cut. But of course Rio had given hers up for a sick ghostbuster. Of course she had.

Cal urged Iumo to take another gulp of tea. "Drink it all. How long ago did you lose Hani?"

He shuddered again and Cal was glad; at least his body was responding to the cold rather than succumbing to it. "Aren't he... with you?"

"No, bud," said Cal, gently as she was able. "I just found you, remember? You're the one who told me you lost him."

"We need to bring him lower," said Anja. She was watching Iumo's eyes and the stiffness of his movements. "Wait much longer and he won't be able to move under his own steam. Got to get him to thicker air, closer to the traversairs."

"Okay," said Cal, but as Anja clipped herself to Iumo's harness to short rope him down the step, she hesitated in the alcove. Was that a cry on the wind?

"It's probably-" Anja called, but Cal ignored her, even though Anja was probably right.

The voice was not of someone living.

Cal hadn't realized how high they'd made it; up to the ridge that climbers called the Maidenhead. It was marked by a rough heap of rocks piled over a long-dead climber on the side of the trail. The cairn hadn't held up against years of howling weather, and scraps of fabric peeked between icy gaps; through one, a shredded glove revealed a single white finger.

The ghost it belonged to stood on the ridge and wept.

Cal took no notice because huddled beside the cairn were two figures, heads bowed.

One was Hani, chin tucked to his chest, the scarf his husband had sent with him still wrapped around his throat. He was holding a smaller figure, the scrappy acolyte girl from the monastery, the one who could hang by her toes and had bragged about the demons she'd banished.

The ice was inches thick on their faces.

Cal let out a sob and slumped to her knees. The girl - Jaine, Cal remembered - had her fingers wrapped around amber prayer beads. There was a burnt twig in the alcove behind her knees. Her nose had already turned black, and her eyes were open, pupils fixed and dilated. She couldn't have been more than eighteen.

Hani was braced behind the girl, his shoulders hunched like he was trying to fold around her. Despite the thick hoar of frost, wisps of his hair had escaped his hood and were blowing, gingery and ragged, around his face. Choking, Cal reached out, cupping a mittened hand around his pale cheek, unable to bear leaving him frozen over like a portrait behind glass. She chipped at the ice, knowing the memory of his face would haunt her worse than any ghost; knowing too that she would memorize it even if it killed her. It was the least she could do for his husband when she brought the news.

The ice around his lips splintered. A puff of mist rose on the air before being whipped away on the wind and Cal gasped. She could see Hani's eyes now.

He blinked.

The plan had been to make it back to Camp Three, stabilize Iumo and Hani, radio down to base for a helicopter, then turn around and head back up for Rio and the others. An expedition bound folk closer than any blood tie, and Cal should know; of her four siblings, she was only on speaking terms with one. Hachi and Hani had been the ones to bring her champagne when she got her residency assignment. Tasi, the tall exorcist with the braids who'd only known Cal a week, had held her feet against her bare stomach to warm them one night at Base when Cal had forgotten her boot warmers.

You didn't leave family behind, and yet that was exactly what Cal did.

She sat in the tent the traversairs had erected, listened to the wind scream, and only barely restrained herself from screaming back. The storm had worsened as soon as they'd made it to camp, their O_2 was dangerously low and they would need a resupply from another team hiking up to meet them before they could ascend. Cal wasn't Search and Rescue. She was the expedition's doctor, and the place she was needed was where there were patients.

There was plenty to do. There was the lukewarm water she was carefully working over Iumo's hands, and the hyperbaric chamber Hani had been in for the last hour. There were injections to administer to counteract the edema in their lungs, and she couldn't hide her relief when Hani twitched and Iumo cursed her out for jabbing it into their hips. "This probably means you won't lose your ass."

"Tragedy prevented," murmured Iumo, and she started to pat dry his hands so that she could bandage them.

It was only once both he and Hani had sunk into a fitful doze that Cal let herself despair.

She sat in the corner, head in her hands, sleeping bag around her shoulders, and let the tears drip onto the polyester. Anja was outside, talking to the traversairs, and Cal knew she was fatigued from the exorcism and the arduous trip down; knew that she should go out and shout the woman into at least an hour of sleep.

Instead, Cal flicked her radio on and off the way Anja thumbed her prayer beads, and listened to the static.

"Cal?" said the radio. A snow-soft whisper, warm and intimate as a hand on her shoulder.

"*Rio.*" Cal rose to her knees, sleeping bag slipping, thumb jabbing the radio. "Rio! Can you hear me?"

Static. Was that a whisper? She could swear Rio was on the other side of the tent wall, that she'd spoken right into Cal's ear.

"Sorry," said Anja outside the tent flap. "Sorry, I was - Wanted to check in on how the boys are doing. Sorry, that was me."

But Cal would know the difference between Rio's whisper and Anja's even if there were only two molecules of oxygen left in the world, and she surged out of the tent, slipping as her boot liners hit the packed snow.

"I heard her." She spun wildly on her heel and over-balanced. Only Anja's grasp at her elbow kept her from hitting the snow

chin first and Cal bit her tongue as she was jerked upright. "I heard her, she's-"

Cal cast her eyes about frantically, as if the swirling snow and implacable headwalls around them offered any answers. Anja glanced around too, uneasy. Their gazes found the northwest corner of camp at the same time, and Anja's hand went tight on Cal's arm.

There was a figure there, wind tossing its sandy hair. Red mittens, red boots, a black snowsuit. A mouth, opened in an anguished cry.

It wore Rio's clothes, but it had no face.

"Rio!" Cal screamed, but no sound came out.

Anja's arm was tight around her waist, holding her back, but Cal pulled away with animal strength, her feet skidding on the ice. She threw herself towards Rio, answering the wail with a wail of her own, and it was only when Anja brought her down that she stopped moving, stopped fighting.

The figure was gone.

She was feet from where it had been. Had she reached it, she would have been balanced on a black ice precipice, beyond which the cwm dropped away a thousand feet or more.

"It was Rio," rasped Cal, blood leaking from her mouth.

"It was a ghost," said Anja, very gently for someone lying with all her weight on Cal's back.

They were both right.

The knowledge of it threw Cal reeling into an agony too savage to endure, and she was unconscious before her head hit the snow.

Her dreams were all of Rio.

Not of that cold, dead, scratching thing pulling itself out of a crevasse, stumbling on broken legs, mouth yawning open onto nothing.

She dreamed of their apartment, tiny and sun-littered, thirty minutes from the hospital, ten from the climbing gym, with the pullup bar installed in the bedroom door frame. Rio would never walk under it without doing a set. She'd never walk past Cal without kissing the top of her head and sliding a hand into Cal's back pocket. Rio's hands with their split nails and calluses, Rio's cackling jaybird laugh and the way she threw her whole body into it like a dive, Rio's mouth, always quirking up at the corners.

"Cal," Rio whispered, in the soft voice she saved for regrets. She'd used it when Cal screamed at her about the cheating. She hadn't when Cal begged her not to climb before the storm because the only other woman in Rio's life that mattered was her Bride. "Hey, Cal, hey baby. It wasn't your fault. You're my anchor, girl. My fixed line. You know I'll always come back to you."

Cal woke to the taste of blood in her mouth, a cough in her chest, and a bleary, high-altitude headache. Also to snoring, and the heat of another body pressed against hers. Anja smelled as bad as Cal probably did, but there was an animal comfort in the closeness of another body and she didn't move away.

Freeing her hand from the sleeping bag so she could check her watch woke Anja, who snorted, rolled over and explained gruffly, "You were shivering by the time I got you in here. And I didn't trust you not to wake up and go throw yourself off the cwm."

"Thanks," Cal said, not especially grateful. The drop would have been easier. Or staying in this sleeping bag forever. But she had to get up, step into the cold, check on her surviving friends, climb a mountain no one ought to climb, and follow a ghost. Her ex-girlfriend and now ex-everything else.

The dim light of a solar lantern flattened Anja's face into a mask. The mountain had weathered her plain features even plainer, and under a short cap of lusterless black hair, her eyes were as black as her mountain's rock, sharp and unyielding, set deep in her face. Her mouth, though, was surprisingly soft. "You loved her."

Past tense. Cal ducked her head, breaking eye contact in case she started crying. "The last thing I said to her was- it wasn't even, 'I hate you,' or 'I never want to see you again.' I said, 'I fucking hate your mom's cooking'. And if we hadn't had that stupid fight..." If Cal had climbed with her, instead of sulking back in camp, then Cal could have told her to turn back sooner, told her to keep her oxygen and stop being a dumbass-

"The storm wouldn't have blown in?" Anja asked, implacable.

Cal shifted so her whole face was pressed to Anja's shoulder and her voice came out muffled, barely audible. "Let me wallow."

"You're too sensible for that."

"You don't know me."

"Pssh." Anja's hand slid away, back into the bag before the cold stole all the warmth from it. "Varga I understand, and those boys defrosting in the other tent. But what the hell are *you* doing this for?"

There were a thousand answers to that. Cal had always said, 'Because someone has to be designated driver,' when people asked, so that Rio would laugh and clap her shoulder.

You courted the Bride because some part of you wanted her more than you feared the fall, and that was something Cal had understood since med school. Since she'd stitched close a gash gouged by a climber's rebounding ice axe and Rio had grinned at her with bloody teeth and asked what she was doing later. "Why did you become a priest?"

"I was a guide for a while, until I saw what it was doing to the mountain. Saw what it was doing to the people." Cal could feel the weight of her gaze like a physical touch. "But the truth is I *missed* this. I know how much Neverfall's hurting, I can feel the pain grow like a tumor every meter we go up. I got myself convinced that coming up here, easing her as much as I could, was the right thing to do, but part of me jumped at the excuse."

"You've freed three ghosts and prevented three more." Cal remembered Anja's gentleness with the ghost in the whiteout. Her concern for Iumo and Hani. Her warm chest pressed against Cal's back. "I think you're doing this for the right reasons. Listen, I'm going back up as soon as the wind lifts, but you don't have to come. It was selfish to make you do this much."

Anja grunted and, looking up, Cal saw lantern light reflected in the black depths of her eyes. "If we find people, you aren't getting them down alone. If we find ghosts, well, that's why I'm up here. Might as well make it count."

Because the mountain had a cruel sense of humor, the morning dawned clear and beautiful.

It was a perfect day for summiting and groups were already setting out for the top, laden with warm clothes and fresh oxygen and everything that could have kept Rio alive had she encountered it soon enough. Cal wondered if the group ahead would find the bodies first, or if Rio and Tasi and Hachi were scattered to the four directions, tossed from the step or buried beneath blown snow. It could be years before their bones were revealed.

In the long night of her grief, Cal had tamped the loss down until it was like the numbness in her toes, pressed to the front of her boots. She knew that if she pressed too hard the pain would come, but for now, she could stumble forward, moving only a little more stiffly than usual. Once she descended to the valley she would stretch her feet to the fire and let the pain rise through her.

But here and now there was only air for one obsession at a time.

"The thing is," said Cal, and stopped. Anja looked up.

The thing was that they might never find Rio's body, or Hachi's, or the girl. They might never find their spirits, either - Ghosts crowded the slopes, but without the minds that had once contained them they were nothing but those last impressions of life. Nothing but panic and confusion and regret, and sometimes that drove them into tents and through radio frequencies, and sometimes they stayed in their ravines, waiting for others to join them. Sometimes they lay under the snow, whispering. Sometimes they blew away on the wind. They didn't come to you when you sought them.

There were *hundreds* of them.

She and Anja could never get rid of them all, not the way they had been doing it. Not one by one in painstaking ritual, finding their names, accepting their grief, showing them the way out. It would be a gargantuan undertaking. It would drive them mad long before they made a dent in the spectral mass.

They'd been fools to think this could work.

"The thing is," said Cal, "that Rio would never leave the mountain." When she saw Anja's mouth open, she went on to curtail her. "She wasn't a holy woman, not literally wed to it like you, but she might as *well* have been. She dreamed of it every night, talked about it every minute. She failed the summit four times before she managed it, and each time I asked if she was done, she looked at me like I was crazy. Was she done with the mountain? It wasn't done with *her*. It was like how some people are with drink, or how some people are with -"

"Lovers," said Anja.

"Yes," said Cal. "Even if we found - her body," her voice caught and cracked, "her spirit wouldn't leave. Her spirit wants the mountain. And Sister, she's not the only one."

Anja sat back and squinted up towards the peak, where the snow and mist streamed out like a veil.

"Climbers ain't regular souls," said Cal, quoting Iumo's favorite saying. "They're going to be hard to shake from your lady."

"Good I'm not a jealous lover." Anja put her hands in her armpits and huffed out a breath. "So. What then? If my bones and herbs and beads aren't enough for your dead climbers, what is? What do you propose, Dr. Bridges?"

"A relationship takes two," said Dr. Bridges, watching the veil break apart in morning winds, "And so does a breakup."

They climbed in silence.

With every crunch of her crampons, Cal expected to see Rio. A corpse or a ghost or Rio alive and coughing blood and lymph, or laughing and telling her to hurry.

Hani hadn't said anything about Hachi when Cal checked in before beginning the climb - still too spaced out by the cold, the thin air, and what she hoped wasn't brain damage. Iumo knew they weren't looking for the living any longer, but had only clapped her shoulder with his good hand and said he hoped Mama Mountain gave them a break.

She did. The weather held.

"To the summit?" Cal had asked, and Anja had shaken her head.

"It'll work better lower, and not only because we'll have more chance of being alive for it. Up past the Maidenhead, where the ground levels. As long as we're into the death zone, that should be high enough."

A part of Cal wanted to argue. Wanted to be sure it worked. Wanted to summit. She choked it back like bile and focused on keeping her fingers nimble and her respirator clear of ice.

She slipped once, foot sliding free of its hold, and for a moment and the fear rose in her stomach as she dropped, only to be brought up short with the clank of her ascender catching and a bruising jolt from her harness. Above her on the ropes, Anja peered down and Cal, panting into her mask, shot her a quick thumbs up.

After yesterday's climb, this was almost relaxing. The worst had happened. It was already too late. Death was immutable.

But the world beyond was not. Up on the Maidenhead, above the cairn where they'd found Hani and left poor Jaine beneath another mound of stones, Anja pressed her palms together, beads wrapped loose around her wrists.

Up here, the spell caught even quicker than it had before. The world went black and soundless almost before the flames caught Anja's herbs. The midnight plane wavered like a mirage, and Anja grunted with effort.

Magic had never been Cal's forte, but Anja had talked her through the basics. Magic was wanting things, and one thing Rio had taught Cal was how to want.

Cal wanted the mountain. Rio's conquest, Anja's bride, with her veil of glittering ice, Neverfall in all her majesty and treachery. There were lovelier mountains, more technical climbs, but they paled to Neverfall, whose weight distorted the world around her, drew priests and climbers and nobodies with something to prove. She collected ghosts like notches on the bedpost.

They no longer stood upon a black plain. The mountain rose around them, dark rock and pale snow.

Anja rose too. She got to her feet, tossing her hood back and pushing her goggles up. She stood, bare-headed and bare-handed before the echo of her mountain bride. She spoke, as she had to the ghosts, in gentle tones. But her words were layered with a tenderness that made Cal blink and look away.

"Tell me what went wrong," said Anja, speaking to her goddess. "Tell me how you died."

The answer came to them not in words or visions, but in knowledge that filled every crevice of their consciousness. Cal knew the mountain's answer because for that beating moment, she *was* the mountain.

She died under boots. She died with footsteps on her back tearing the snowcaps from her flanks. She died under ice axes and pitons, strangled in rope, transfixed by steel. She died in the inexorable fall of pebbles from her ridgelines, and in avalanches that streamed down her face from those who fell too hard or shouted too loudly.

She died buried in refuse. She died beneath the tonnage of oxygen tanks and plastic wrappers and frozen human shit; beneath piss-streaked snow and bloodstained ice. She died beneath abandoned tents and forsaken fuel canisters and a thousand lost boots.

She died under their agony. Under the weight of a thousand broken spirits and abandoned dreams, under regret and guilt and disappointment. She died beneath their suffering, her glaciers soaked with the fear and pain of a thousand final moments. She died as they died, their bodies frozen to her sides like lost children seeking a warmth she could never offer. She died under the tromp of their boots, and then again under the restlessness of their spirits.

She died of their want.

Tears rolled down Cal's cheeks, and here, beyond the wind's grasp, they did not freeze. They traced hot fingers down her face and throat, and wet her lips and collar. The sadness wrapped itself around her very bones.

Anja didn't weep. "Darlin'," she said to the mountain. "Tell me how you lived."

She lived stretching for the sky. She lived leaning into the jetstream; tossing a veil of ice from her peak to watch it dance on the current of the world. She lived to carve her name against the blue. She lived for the stars that hung just out of reach and for the storms that broke themselves on her summits.

She lived for the ice that cracked her veins and split seracs from her like sloughing skin. She lived for snows that kept her secrets, buried her scars. She lived for the high loneliness, for the silence, for the company of eagles and the solitude of chasms. She lived desiring the cap of the world, the crown of the sky; she lived, seeking, wanting.

So had her ghosts.

The mountain kept what you gave her. Corpses and prayers and empty cans and *love*. The kind of love that crushed and froze and tethered. The kind of love that Cal knew all about.

Wet faced, her toes just warm enough to hurt in her boots, Cal stepped forward and stretched wide her arms.

"Great one," she said. "Let them go. Cut the line."

Behind her, through the door they had opened in the highness of the death zone, came the ghosts. They clustered at Cal's back, pressing close with their tattered Gore-Tex and black cheeks. They had flung themselves towards the sky that they might fall somewhere mighty. They took and took, and gave and gave, until all that was left were their shattered spirits and the echo of the mountain on a black plain.

Anja looked back and took Cal's hand, pulling her free of the press. She held it tight as she looked back up at the shadow mountain, and Cal braced herself against Anja's side. "Well, Mama? Will you let them go?"

For one last moment, Cal knew what it was to be the mountain and felt her answer.

Yes.

The ghosts streamed around Cal and Anja like rapids around strainers. They coursed and converged and made their way towards the peak of a mountain whose air was as thin as they were and whose spires were no sharper than their own fingers.

As the ranks of ghosts clanked on cramponed feet towards their release, Cal could have sworn that one stopped on its path and turned for a moment to look back at her. Red boots, red gloves, and a lean body all in black.

Cal raised a hand; pressed fingers to her lips.

The ghost caught her kiss in one red-glove, then turned and carried it with her to the summit.

The radio blared. "Kharo, this is base camp, do you copy?"

Kharo's answer came with a crackle of static and Cal flicked to the next channel. She'd been checking every couple of hours, but so far the only voices on the airwaves belonged to the living.

It wouldn't last. It couldn't. The mountain couldn't not be what it was, and the climbers couldn't either.

"You're brooding," Iumo rumbled, and she sighed and turned the radio off. He was sitting beside her in a canvas chair that groaned beneath his weight, feet stretched out towards the firepit as he ate a bowl of instant noodles.

"You're very cheerful for a man with eight fingers," Cal said, hanging the kettle on its hook over the flames; the noodles smelled amazing.

"When you offer the Bride your hand, you can't go complaining if she doesn't give it all back."

Fingers were the least of what she wouldn't give back. Hani had been airlifted to a proper hospital; his husband was with him, and Hachi's girlfriend, and Cal had left them keeping sleepless vigil around the bed.

While her friends healed, Cal had walked the cloisters with the Master Channeller, past the new mosaic, and told her that her students had been brave, a credit to her school.

She'd called Rio's mother.

She'd warmed her toes until the pain closed around her like a whiteout.

Now, she dumped an extra packet of seasoning into the bowl and ate her noodles.

Above them was the peak, unshadowed, crowned in sunlight. Awe, horror, grief and love all seemed much too big and still too small for all the mountain was to her now.

But it was a beautiful view, and Cal leaned back in her chair to appreciate it.

She found it blocked by blue robes draped over broad shoulders.

"Word is you're trekking out tomorrow," said Anja, looking down at her.

Iumo could move with a cat's grace when he chose, and he slipped from his chair so quietly Cal almost didn't catch him leaving.

"My flight's booked," Cal said. "I've been looking for you to say goodbye." The other skybrides at the monastery had shaken their heads when she'd asked for Anja, given her the same somber stares they had the first time she'd passed.

"I've had penance." Anja sounded embarrassed.

"Penance?" Cal sat upright in her chair. "But you saved everyone! You saved your Lady!"

"The Reverend Mother's set in her ways. Takes 'Don't climb the holy mountain' as less a guideline, more a commandment." Anja shook off the embarrassment as she stamped snow off her boots. "You've more sense than her, for all you're a heathen rabbit of a woman."

"I'll miss you too," Cal told her and meant it. Bonds formed fast and tight when you had to hang your life from them. Anja reminded her of Rio, a little. A Rio whose common sense tempered her reckless courage. The kind of woman she'd always thought Rio could become if Cal dug her nails in and hung on long enough.

"Will you be back?" Anja asked, and Cal couldn't quite tell what she wanted the answer to be.

Neverfall lived, seeking, wanting. But Cal knew what she wanted now.

"Not for the climb," she said, and Anja smiled like sunlight on snow.

Denali Stannard is the transatlantic literary partnership of Denali Hussin and Megan Stannard, represented by Saritza Hernandez of the Andrea Brown Literary Agency. Their debut work, an urban fantasy trilogy, is currently out on submission.

Denali Hussin, the top half of Denali Stannard, has worked the past decade in sustainability, climate change, and science communication. She writes The Stoop Gallants, *a twice-weekly fantasy webcomic. She lives on the Rocky Mountain side of the ocean.*

Megan Stannard is the back end of the literary pantomime horse that is Denali Stannard. She is a conservationist who dabbles in sword fighting, horse riding, and anything else that will make her a better writer (or fantasy protagonist. You know, if it ever comes up). She lives on the Hampstead Heath side of the ocean.

Follow their work at denalistannard.com or on social media @denalistannard.

Steampunk
Article by Mark Bilsborough

We love steampunk. All that Victorian retro-chic fantasy sci fi nonsense with cool designs, fast moving action, zeppelins everywhere and clockwork people, all with a whispered hint of magic and a heavy dose of high steam adventure. In fact we like it so much that we're publishing a steampunk anthology – Runs like Clockwork – out just in time for Christmas.

So what is steampunk, and why are we so excited to be publishing some? Put bluntly, it's Victoriana science run by clockwork and coal, or science gone modern by another route. And it's everywhere, from books to comics to films to TV to games to cosplay to conventions to that weird sepia coloured long coat, pith helmet and flying goggles ensemble currently being modelled on the stranger end of the high street.

But despite all its retro styling and feet firmly planted in the 19th Century, steampunk is actually pretty new and stemmed from cyberpunk in the 1980s – a decidedly tech-heavy futuristic offshoot of science fiction made popular by William Gibson, Bruce Sterling and others. Steampunk author Kevin Wayne Jeter wrote to *Locus* magazine back in 1987 suggesting the term 'steam-punk' to describe novels such as his and similar hard to pigeonhole work by Tim Powers and James Blaylock. The name stuck and, fittingly, has been handsomely retrofitted to embrace work by actual Victorian era writers like HG Wells' clockwork contraption in *The Time Machine* and Shelley's mad scientist *Frankenstein* are the template for more recent wild imaginings, and writers from Pullman to Priest and Powers have not let us down.

Since then, full on steampunk and steampunk inspired novels have won all sorts of awards and have steadily edged more conventional fare right off the bookshelves.

On our screens, too. *Wild Wild West*, a 1999 movie adaptation of a decidedly odd 1960's TV series, sets the tone. Mechanical spiders in the desert in the Old West chasing Will Smith in a Stetson. Then there's *Mortal Engines* (2018 – from a Philip Reeves book) with mobile cities in a post apocalypse world, and *The League of Extraordinary Gentlemen* (2003) based on the infinitely better Alan Moore comic book, with Sean Connery and a slightly bemused cast fighting Victorian terrorists with the aid of the Invisible Man, My Hyde, Dorian Gray and other shamelessly appropriated characters.

TV, too. We've got the adaptation of Philip Pullman's *His Dark Materials* from the BBC, set in an unworldly, magic-infused Oxford, and some mighty fine streaming fare, such as Cara Delavigne and Orlando Bloom in *Carnival Row*, where the Fae are refugees in a Victorian gothic nightmare and the recent *Shadow and Bone*, set in a reimagined, magic-infused Russian Empire.

Steampunk's rules are loose and fluid and it's more about the style, approach and colour palette than a strict insistence on a Victorian London setting. Some of the best steampunk novels are almost timeless, such as Cheri Priest's *Clockwork Century* series, set just after the American Civil War or Jeanette NG's *Under The Pendulum Sun*, set in an alt-history landscape where the fae have their own country. They are fantasies and the fantastical, so don't be surprised if a little magic, or the hint of it, creeps out from time to time.

Much of what shapes the perception of steampunk is stimulated by its enthusiastic supporters. Pre-pandemic, steampunk conventions were everywhere, such as the Asylum convention, held annually in historic Lincoln (UK), allowing fans everywhere to dress in outlandish costumes. Victorian clothing, airships and mechanical men everywhere!

If this is a fad, it's an enduring one. Its mix of high adventure, strong characters, weird reimaginings and a hint of darkness is certainly compelling and it's now firmly established as a fantasy sub-genre. Steampunk novels are winning Hugo awards. The future truly is the past,

Steampunk newbie? Start here:

- **William Gibson and Bruce Sterling's** *The Difference Engine* arguably kicked steampunk off in the modern era with computers turning up a century before they're supposed to leading to 'steam driven cybernetic engines', 'steam dreadnoughts' and 'calculating cannons'. But is the world ready for such sophisticated – and dangerous - contraptions?

- **Tim Powers'** *Anubis Gates* is a time travel romp with a 20th century man, Brendan Doyle, trapped in 1810 and surrounded by weird and dangerous forces. Twisted, evil clowns and dark magic. Street fighters and the London underworld suffuse this high paced 19th Century fantasy – and the great poet Coleridge makes an appearance.

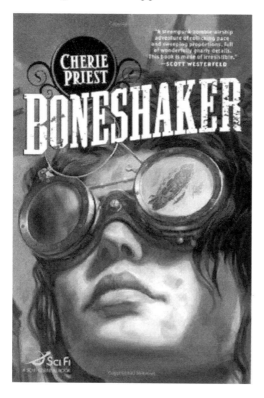

- **Cherie Priest's** *Boneshaker* is the groundbreaking first entry in her Clockwork Century series, set around the American Civil War where in the rush for gold in the Klondike inventor Leviticus Blue creates a mighty machine, the boneshaker, to break through Alaskan ice. But things, naturally, go wrong, and something terrible is unleashed on the infernal machine's test run in Seattle.

- **Stephen Baxter's** *Anti-Ice* what-if's a new energy source found by the Victorians in Antarctica – strong enough to power all manner of contraptions on land, on sea – and even to the moon. But power can be used for many purposes and anti-ice can be as much a source of destruction as it is development. Will good prevail?

- **Paul Di Fillipo's** *The Steampunk Trilogy* comprises three short alt-history 19th century novels, with Queen Victoria replaced by a clone, sea monsters threatening Massachusetts and a time and space hopping Emily Dickinson swapping stories with Walt Whitman and Allen Ginsberg,

- **Cassandra Clare's** *The Infernal Devices*: plunges her readers into a, Victorian London brimming with vampires, demons and warlocks and their clockwork creations, bent on ruling the Empire. These novels, forerunners to her *Mortal Instruments* series, follow the Shadowhunters in their fight against the darkness and their powerful enemies in the demonic Pandemonium Club..

- **Nisl Shawl's** *Everfair* An ambitious and gripping alt- history set in a 19th century enclave of the Belgian Congo on land bought from King Leopold (and stolen from indigenous people) to form a new country – Everfair – as a safe haven from colonial tyranny. And, of course, there's technology, steampunk style.

This is just a snapshot – steampunk's everywhere these days. We review a couple of steampunk series by two other fine writers – Ian Tregillis and Liesel Schwartz elsewhere in this issue, where you'll find fast paced tales of airship pirates and rebellious clockwork men. Plenty to get you warmed up for our *Runs Like Clockwork* anthology

Happy reading.

We Will Control the Horizontal
Film and TV by **Mark Bilsbborough**

I've often wondered why going out to see a film involves a trip to the cinema in the UK but a trip to the theatre in the US (and, presumably, other places). Though it's a moot question: the cinemas (theatres) have been shut for months and my local fleapit (please tell me you call them that in the States too) has half its sign missing and its windows boarded up.

Apparently there'll be a post-COVID resurgence, if there's ever a post-Covid. Marvel movies aplenty and big blockbusters are promised, but don't bet against more delays, rollbacks and TV releases.

Disney/Marvel finally cracked with *Black Widow* and are following the Warners/DC example and intend to release the much-delayed movie though Disney+ (July 9th). There's a hefty access fee, just like *Wonder Woman 1984*, but at least it's out there, and on limited release on the big screen, if you can find one that's open.

Still, *Black Widow* was in danger of becoming an anachronistic irrelevance so it's nice that it's finally coming out. It's firmly tied to the Phase 3 movies that culminated in *Avengers: Endgame* and that's so *yesterday*. Best then to see it now on the small screen than to wait until all the new and shiny Marvel TV shows consign it to history.

DC's most recent small screen big movie was the long awaited (and much hyped) Zach Snyder *Justice League* Cut, and at a hefty four hours, maybe it's best to watch it on a device with pause and rewind buttons. Odd project, brief history: Snyder directed the original but left before the final edit for 'personal reasons'. Joss Whedon (Firefly / Buffy / Avengers) swept in to save the day and add a joke or two. Following a so-so release and meh reviews fans agitated for the mythical 'Snyder cut' – and $70 million reshoot dollars later here it is in all its, um, glory.

Plot? Batman gets a few supertypes together (Aquaman, Wonder Woman, Cyborg, The Flash) to fight off the world-destroying Steppenwolf, who's gathering three 'mother boxes' which, together, give him unrivalled power. All very Infinity Stones. Lurking in the background is the memory of Superman, dead and buried in *Batman v Superman: Dawn of Justice* – though, of course, no-one in the comics *really* dies.

Problem is, not much has changed from the reviled Whedon cut. Snyder's version is longer, and there's more backstory (particularly for Cyborg) but there's another one-dimensional bad guy (the Thanos-lite Darkseid) and that makes two one-dimensional bad guys too many. You'd expect a four-hour movie to be a bit slow, and you won't be disappointed. Plus there's an inexplicable epilogue featuring a few nods to what might have happened if Warner had trusted Snyder with more indifferent movies. In one the Martian Manhunter flies in, exchanges small talk with Bruce Wayne then flies off. In another, Batman has a long conversation with Jared Leto's Joker in some post-apocalyptic nightmare which has zero to do with the movie. It smacks of indulgence, but split into more manageable chunks it should keep comic book movie fans happy until more original fare appears, like the long awaited Robert Pattison version of *The Batman*.

Some interesting things have found their way onto TV, though, thanks to Netflix and the other streamers. My favourite of the recent releases is the lavish *Shadow and Bone*, based on the popular YA fantasy novels by Leigh Bardugo, who once described them as 'Tzarpunk' There's definitely a steampunk feel to this fast paced fantasy romance, set somewhere vaguely Russian with vaguely 19th century tech plus a large dollop of magic. The province of Ravka has been split into East and West by nightmarish, magical barrier called the Shadow Fold, plagued by flying monsters and only passable with luck, caution, ingenuity and preferably accompanied by someone with supernatural abilities. A young woman, Alina Starov, discovers she's a 'grisha', with the power to create light. Could she be the key to destroying the dark Shadow Fold? Bad guys are after her, though, and her first love (Mal) is gone – will she fall for the powerful allure of the Shadow Summoner? All eight episodes on Netflix now – highly recommended.

The Falcon and the Winter Soldier recently

concluded its run over on Disney+, and if you were looking for signposts for the direction Marvel is taking as it enters its Phase 4 the signs are encouraging. The short run episodic format seems to suit these characters – over six tightly packed episodes, director Kari Skogland powers through a complex plotline involving super-powered terrorists, a new, flawed Captain America and a surprising new take on Baron Zemo, and at the same time oversees some significant character developments as Sam Wilson (The Falcon) and Bucky Barnes (The Winter Soldier) come to terms with their post -*Endgame* lives. It feels like one of the later Captain America films given more space and a lower profile – more *Jason Bourne* than *Iron Man* – and it works. It's especially pleasing to see actors from the films reprising their pasts: this time it feels like Marvel might actually follow through with their intentions of properly integrating their film and TV projects. I hope so – earlier promises with *Agents of Shield* came to nothing as the TV series disappeared into its own parallel universe, but this time Marvel supremo Kevin Feige has overall control of everything – and the early signs are very encouraging.

The second series of *For All Mankind* is now on Apple TV+. Easy to miss this one in our multi-platform world, but it's destined to become a classic and deserves wide

exposure. Two ten-episode seasons so far, created by Ronald D Moore (of *Battlestar Galactica* and *Outlander* fame) it tells the alt-history story of the Russians landing on the moon first. Season two picks up in the 1980s, with a repurposed Skylab serving as the core of an American moon base and the Soviets lurking on the other side of a mineral-rich crater. Tensions rise as the two superpowers jostle for control. For all its interesting speculation, *For All Mankind* is very character driven, closely following the lives and mishaps of the astronauts, their families and the Houston team. It's sometimes hopeful, often scary and very engaging. Importantly, it feels credible. Season three is teased as fast-forwarding to a Mars landing. Can't wait.

Lastly, two films recently released on Netflix. *Stowaway* carries on the Mars theme with a three man mission that becomes derailed when the crew discovers a

stowaway – and some mission-critical damage. It's a tightly plotted engaging story with a good mix of action and intrigue. Toni Collette is excellent as mission commander but the impressive Anna Kendrick steals the show as the doctor who has some very hard choices to make. Tense and satisfying – recommended.

Then there's George Clooney's *Midnight Sky*, from last year, where Clooney survives virtually alone on a dead earth, helping the crew of a deep space mission come to terms with their home's destruction and, hopefully, save their mission. Clooney at his best and well worth watching.

More in the pipeline: new *Walking Dead , Star Trek Strange New World, Doctor Who, Loki, Foundation, The Witcher, Station Eleven, The Lord of the Rings* and more. Most if not all of these shows should debut later this year, lockdown permitting. And of course we'll cover them right here.

Chronicles of Light and Shadow:

A Conspiracy of Alchemists
A Clockwork Heart
Sky Pirates

Leisel Schwarz

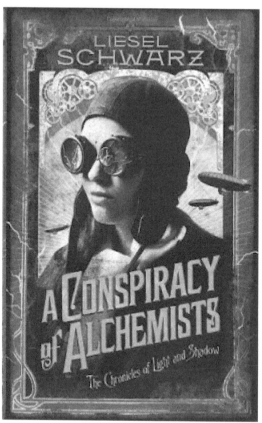

A Conspiracy of Alchemists is the debut novel by British writer Leisel Schwarz, the first in a series of the *Chronicles of Light and Shadow*.

Fairies are mentioned in the first sentence, vampires in the third. Normally I'd stop right there but reviewers don't get that option so I carried on. I'm glad I did, because this is a well written, well constructed tale with engaging characters and a confident, articulate style. It's steampunk, so don't expect high art, but it works and it's entertaining.

This is the story of Eleanor Chance, who flies airships for a living, and who has a destiny she resists for most of the book. She agrees to take on a passenger and a mysterious, sealed cargo from Paris to London. The passenger, Marsh, is of course more than he seems and the cargo is much in demand. So much so, that they have to leave Paris in a hurry, without flight clearance, and with the French police shooting frantically at them.

When they get to England they find that Elle's father has been abducted so they begin a chase across Europe in a gyrocopter chased by pirates in airships, on the Orient Express by thugs and nightwalkers (vampires) and through the streets of Constantinople by just about everybody. It all builds to a crescendo where things could get decidedly nasty.

Two things drive this series. One is the narrative, which pushes the action well, ramping up tension nicely but still giving space for characterisation. The second is the budding romance between Elle and March, telegraphed right from the start but holding the novel together throughout. This is very much a steampunk romance, but don't let that put you off. The mix is actually quite endearing.

The underlying theme of the series is the fight between the 'Light' and the 'Shadow', which on the surface sounds like straight good and evil. But some of the good guys – Marsh for instance, and the delightful nightcrawler Loisa – are attached to Shadow and the bad guys (the alchemists) are, I believe, aligned with the Light. Shadow is all about magic and Light about science and invention. As one rises the other wanes. By 1903, when the book is set, science and industry have reduced the power and influence of magic and Light and Shadow are out of balance. The whole system is normally held together by the Oracle, but when the book opens there isn't a proper Oracle overseeing things. And when one starts to emerge, both Light and Dark want her to shore up their own position.

The fuzzy nature of Light and Shadow is important in making this more than just a steampunk by numbers story. Characters flip from good to bad to good to somewhere in the middle and there's lots if misdirection to keep you on your toes.

The first book is a bit uneven, though. There's a prologue of sorts written by an absinthe fairy (really) which is misleading in tone and then the book properly kicks off chapter one with a line I wish I'd written: 'the opium den above the café du Aleix smelled of clove incense and oblivion'. Great line, but still a misdirect, because the book's not about opium or oblivion, just as it's not about vampires and fairies. After a while the style loosens up and the story proper emerges, but for a few chapters the style seems a little forced, as if the text has been through a few too many revisions. It really settles down about half way through, and from that point on the story is a delight, so stick with it.

So, good worldbuilding, and a strong narrative. It's gothic, it's steampunk and it's well written.

The second volume, A Clockwork Heart, has Elle married to a warlock and devoting her life to keep dark shadows in their place. But then the warlock husband – Marsh – somehow manages to acquire a clockwork heart – and things get very steampunk.

By the time the last volume in the trilogy, *Sky Pirates*, was released, the author had,

apparently, become 'the high-priestess of steampunk' at least according to the *Independent*, which will come as an unwelcome surprise to Cherie Priest.

The series continues the adventures of Elle Chance, a posh and slightly accident prone airship pilot who in previous novels became the 'Oracle', which rather than being a person who knows stuff (she doesn't) is the person who acts as a bridge between the world of Shadow and the world of Light. Also included are various sky pirates (hence the name), an ex-husband to track down, an old ally turned mean and powerful and a

rather large two-headed dog with murderous intent.

Elle's ship, the Water Lily is attacked and her friend, Gertrude, killed, leaving behind a treasure map. For some reason Elle decides to make her peace with the captain of the ship who attacked her, Dashwood, and becomes part of his crew. Together they hunt for the treasure, though Elle's motives are information: she wants to find a way to rescue her husband from his permanently wraith-like state in the Shadow Realm. This leads to numerous scrapes, a bit of steaminess, pith helmets (yes, really) and lots of pirates.

There's plenty of action here – it starts with an action sequence as Elle gets away from desert raiders and then uses her magic Oracle powers to whip up a deadly sandstorm in order to rescue some other people. That's the pattern for the book, and the action leads Elle and Dashwood to the jungles of Cambodia and some difficult decisions. There are plenty of unresolved plot threads too, so a sequel seems inevitable.

Alchemy Wars:

The Mechanical
The Rising
The Liberation

Ian Tregilis,

Every time a new batch of books arrives there's always one that stands out. It usually isn't the one I expect, and it certainly by rights shouldn't have been a steampunky sounding thing called *The Mechanic*. Yet there it was. An absolute delight, all the more so because it was so surprising.

The book is set in an alternate 1926 where the Dutch Empire rules most of the world, the French are corralled near the St Lawrence river and the Pope is in exile in Quebec. There is no United States, no Great Britain and no serious threat to Dutch superiority. The reason is that Holland, centuries before, mixed alchemy with clockwork and produced sentient mechanical men, bound to obedience by pain-backed compulsions, or 'geas', weaved into their consciousnesses.

The French haven't given up, though. Berenice, inheritor of the title and role of 'Talleyrand', attempts to unravel the secrets of the rogue mechanical locked in her dungeon in Marseilles-in-the-West, hoping to discover why some mechanicals can gain free will.

Rogues are rare: officially they don't exist. Officially mechanicals have no souls, no humanity. But when a servitor, Jax, finds he's no longer bound by painful geas and able to exercise free will, the story moves swiftly into an action packed exploration of the nature of humanity, free will, compulsion and the soul. Protestant Dutch are up against Catholic French, and their differences vividly colours the book. That and Tregillis' fantastic characters: the very human Mechanical Jax, the French spy and cleric Pastor Visser, the scheming Berenice Charlotte de Mornay-Perigord and many others, who are frequently not what they seem.

One of the book's strengths is that despite its heavy philosophical underpinnings – Spinoza has a central role to play, for instance – this novel never flags. It's full of movement, packed with action and has an engaging plot, full of mysteries and twists and turns. The three point of view characters – Berenice, Jax and Visser, all experience profound and lasting change and their three synchronised tales weave around the central plot in an elegant construction.

In the second volume *The Rising*, war is afoot – the Dutch and their 'clakker' army prepare to attack Marseilles-In-The-West (in Canada) where the exiled Frenh King is taking a stand. Berenice is out for revenge and the freed clakker – Jax – discovered some uncomfortable truths about himself, the clakker rebels (led by Queen Mab – what could go wrong?) and the dysfunctional, fantastic world he lives in.

The Liberation rounds out Ian Tregilis' "Alchemy Wars" trilogy, and does so with some panache. The usual caveats about reading the first books first apply (you can read reviews elsewhere on this site) since jumping in at the two thirds point will be a) confusing and b) a waste, since there are two other books to enjoy and reading this one first will lead to spoilers.

The basics: this is steampunk. A world where clockwork servants are animated by alchemy and controlled by heavy restrictions, or geas. But then the 'clakkers' break free of their constraints, start to believe they have souls, and begin to turn on their former masters. So this is post-apocalypse, steampunk-style, in a world where the Dutch and the French have carved things out between them but now face a new, mechanical enemy that has the potential to wipe them all out. The Mechanicals have a Mad Queen Mab stirring them on to ever greater atrocities and misdeeds, from her Northern home in Neverland supported by her grotesquery of 'lost boys'. All very Peter Pan, and this book has a similarly adventurous feel to it. Then there is the mechanical's saviour, Jax, now reborn as Daniel and treated by his followers as a messiah, leading the new free souls of the clakkers to an uncertain future.

Old favourites from the previous books reappear: the foul-mouthed one-eyed Berenice, New France's Talleyrand, or spy supreme, now working with Daniel to restore order. And Anastasia, the Dutch Tunier, or clockmaker's enforcer – ruthless, witty and probably the last credible opposition to Queen Mab's murderous clakkers.

The action takes place on two continents, with Berenice chasing down Queen Mab in North America and Anastasia fighting an increasingly desperate defence against rogue clakkers in The Hague. For the Dutch, the loss of the clakkers means they will need to develop an entirely new way of life – can they survive without servants? Have they gone soft? For the French, who in previous books had been fighting and losing a war with the Dutch, initial relief turns to fear. Only the Dutch had clakker servants: without them, their wartime advantage disappeared. But clakkers don't really differentiate between Dutch humans and French humans. And then – delicious irony – the clakkers find a way to use alchemy to control humans. Only Berenice, Daniel and Anastasia stand between the rogues and genocide.

Liberation is very much about the newly free clakkers coming of age, deciding what kind of creatures they want to be and how they can fit in a world full of their former masters. It provides the rare feat of rounding out the series in a satisfying way and leaving you wanting more. All three books are well executed and fun. Enjoyable.

Inscape

Louise Carey

Set in near-future London, there's been some sort of dystopian meltdown which has left the city shattered but rebuilding. But (like many of us have always believed) there's an almost impenetrable divide between north of the river and the slightly more edgy districts to the south, as different corporations hold each side in their icy, controlling grip (democracy this is most definitely *not*). InTech is in charge in the north and Thoughtfront in the south and there's an uneasy truce between them.

Tantra is a 'CorpWard', orphaned and moulded by InTech to be a highly malleable Agent: a superspy hardwired for loyalty. She's young, but personnel shortages means she's called on while she's still undergoing training on a mission to retrieve data from the Unaffiliated Zone – a no-man's land of anarchy and danger. The story kicks in early with high stakes action: there's another agent in the field, and she's taking out Tantra's team, one by one.

The mission lost, Tantra must make amends and is paired with an older operative, Cole, to regain the lost data files – from behind enemy lines. The cold war has heated up – industrial espionage with deadly consequences has closed the borders ramping up tension and making Tantra's job all but impossible. And then her brain threatens to explode…

What follows is a murky trail of lies, deception, fast moving action and twisting story arc, held together by a strong character journey of self-discovery. Tantra is coming of age and learning that the world she knew and the certainties she felt are twisted inside out – like all strong narratives she isn't the same person at the end as she is in the beginning.

The driving narrative, dystopian setting and engaging characters make this a satisfying read – from mysterious 'directors' who communicate via a mind-wiped 'sleeper' to the tech genius Cole with significant gaps in his memory, Carey's characters are never straightforward.

This book's not perfect – but the force of the storytelling pulls you through any plot holes without too much trouble. There are threads that I'd have preferred were drawn out more – for instance Tantra's relationship with fellow CorpWard Reet is never fully explored – if Reet is under InTech's conditioning, can their relationship be real? And if Tantra has broken her own conditioning, can their relationship be sustained? – but there's a sequel, heavily trailed in the closing pages, so maybe we'll get more there.

This is dystopian espionage cyberpunk, and it's very compelling. Recommended, obviously. And hopefully Louise Carey writes quickly so we don't have to wait too long for the next instalment.

Gallowglass

S. J. Morden

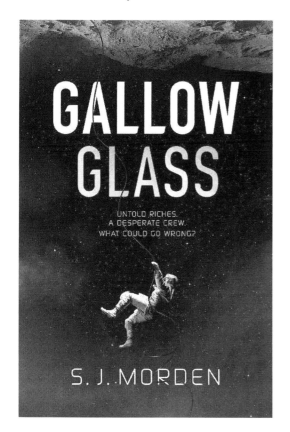

SJ Morden is otherwise published as Simon Morden and is a well-published British writer whose works include the Philip K Dick Award winning *Metrodome* post-apocalyptic novels. He's a PhD-holding Teaching Assistant and, if *Gallowglass* is anything to go by, a mighty fine writer.

Set in near space in the near future the planet is, predictably, falling apart leaving the rich ever richer and the poor scrambling for land that's not under water. As the novel opens, 23 year old Jaap Van der Veerden ('Jack') is attempting to escape from the compound his parents, some of the wealthiest people on the planet, have effectively imprisoned him in. They want to join him in becoming 'transhuman' – effectively immortal – but he's more interested in living a life and doing something useful. Via a series of mishaps and misadventures he ends up as 'Jack Astrogator', getting the crew of a salvage ship alongside an asteroid packed with trillion dollars' worth of iron and other precious metals. The mission brief is to rescue a 'gallowglass' – someone who has staked a claim on the asteroid – and then get the whole pile of rock back Earthwards where it can be broken up and everyone can get rich. But lies, greed, double-crossing and hubris ensue so things don't go *entirely* to plan.

For one thing the 'gallowglass' is a 15 year old girl with a sense of entitlement and a take no prisoners attitude to what she wants. For another, the crew start fighting over the spoils. And accidents will happen…

This is partly redemption story, partly high speed adventure. It's a standalone novel (a rare but welcome occurrence these days) but one I'd happily buy any sequel to. The setting and the timeframe make it *Expanse* territory, though the writing style's more British and the pace and tone are different. It probably shares some genetic material with Ian Mcdonald's excellent *Luna* series, too, which is to say it's in good company and it holds its own.

This book is very easy to read (notwithstanding some overly technical pages describing a shuttle touching down in minimal gravity on a spinning, high velocity object surrounded by slowly rotating space debris). The characters are well drawn and there are some deftly played out choices some of them have to make. There's an interesting parallel set of dilemmas – Jack learns what he'd be prepared to do to give up wealth and fame and some of his crewmates learn just what they'd do to get hold of it. Jack can never truly escape his past, no matter how short he cuts his hair, but how he reconciles himself to it makes for interesting reading.

Gallowglass is a solid, well written near space science fiction story. Recommended.

That's all for now – head over to www.wyldblood.com for more great fiction – see you next time.

Printed in Great Britain
by Amazon